The Professor

Sgt. Bull Cotton

RUSSKY

RUSSKY

George Armor Sentman

DOUBLEDAY & COMPANY, INC.
GARDEN CITY, NEW YORK

Throughout World War II, the 112th Infantry was a standard infantry regiment. There was no 4th Battalion, coded Horseshoe Green. Oboe Company did not exist. The characters in this story are all fictional, and any resemblance to actual persons, living or dead, is purely coincidental.

Library of Congress Catalog Card Number 65–17270
Copyright © 1965 by George Armor Sentman
All Rights Reserved
Printed in the United States of America
First Edition

For Monica and Peter

The Colmar Pocket stuck out like a sore thumb.

It was the last major German bridgehead west of the Rhine.

On January 1, 1945, the Germans had launched a drive in Alsace, co-ordinating it with their gigantic effort in the Ardennes Forest, which has gone down in history as the Battle of the Bulge. The Germans' Alsatian offensive gained some ground, but in the end it failed, leaving behind the Pocket.

This swollen salient stretched fifty miles along the Rhine, and at its point of deepest penetration into Allied territory, about thirty miles west of the Rhine. It was a challenge to the French First Army, the Allied force to which General Eisenhower had given the mission of wiping out the Pocket. The city of Colmar had great meaning for the French, and their First Army grimly prepared to recapture it. But first, the French borrowed strength from the United States Army.

The U. S. Seventh Army lent them the 3d, 36th and 63d Divisions. The U. S. First Army sent the 28th Division, and the 75th. This was heavy, decisive reinforcement. The French, thus strengthened, were ready to attack. On January 20, 1945, pressure against the Pocket began. There was hard fighting along the rim—Adolf Hitler had ordered his 19th Army to stand fast at all costs—but as the Belgian Bulge was reduced, so was the Colmar Pocket. Oddly, the 28th Division front remained quiet.

"Patrol aggressively," Major General Norman "Dutch" Cota ordered, "and wait."

So the GIs of the 28th Bloody Bucket Division patrolled and waited. It was the coldest winter in modern European history, and there were more casualties from frostbite than from bullets. They suffered, but they endured. Originally called the Keystone Division, the 28th had been dubbed "The Iron Division" by General Pershing in World War I, and now, in World War II, it had earned its present nickname, "Bloody Bucket," by spilling its own blood in battle.

The 28th had fought through the Normandy hedgerows; had been the first American division to penetrate Luxemburg in force; had survived a blood bath in the Hürtgen Forest; and had distinguished itself in the Battle of the Bulge. (One regiment, the 112th Infantry, was later to receive a Distinguished Unit Citation for its action in Belgium.) The freezing dogfaces of the 28th wondered why they had been handed this bad deal in Alsace when what they needed was a good long rest, but despite their griping they hadn't lost their spirit. When the whistle blew, they would be ready.

Meanwhile, in a German slave labor camp east of the Rhine, a Russian boy named Pyotr didn't want to wait. He wanted his freedom *now*. One day he was sent west of the Rhine, into the Colmar Pocket itself, to help rebuild a bombed-out bridge.

If only the Americans would attack while I'm here, Pyotr thought, *I might escape from the Germans.*

It was a slim chance, but in wartime strange things happen.

This is the story of what happened to Pyotr. . . .

CONTENTS

RUSSKY

Chapter 1

Pyotr swung his ax hard. The blade bit deep into the slim young pine tree. He yanked the blade free and swung again. A neat wedge of wood fell to the snowy ground. He drew back the ax for another stroke, and then he paused, listening.

"Do you hear it?" he said.

"Hear what?" old Ivan growled.

"The shooting," Pyotr said. "Machine guns, over to the left."

"Of course I hear it," old Ivan said. "I've been hearing it off and on all day long. It doesn't mean anything."

"But—"

"This is a quiet front," old Ivan said patiently. "You can't expect them to start a big battle just to accommodate one boy."

Pyotr lashed out viciously with his ax. This time the blade cut into the trunk far from the mark, and he had to tug at the handle to free it.

"Shooting has to mean *something*," he said.

"They're probably just warming up their weapons," old Ivan said in a weary voice. "Machine guns can easily freeze in weather like this. It's so cold—"

"I know it's cold," Pyotr snapped. "Let's finish with this tree before *we* freeze."

The ax strokes rang out clearly in the thin mountain air, echoing among the steep ridges and valleys. Pyotr chopped twice as fast as old Ivan, and he began to feel almost warm.

"Watch it," old Ivan said. "There she goes."

The tree swayed. Pyotr stepped out of the way of the falling trunk. The tree landed with a hollow boom, sending up a spray of snow. After that, Pyotr hacked at branches while Ivan leisurely lopped off the tapering top of the tree. Minutes later Ivan straightened up with a satisfied grunt.

"There," he said. "Our job is done. Now let's see those lazy Poles drag it down to the bridge."

Pyotr allowed himself a thin smile. The Poles were anything but lazy. It was just that old Ivan had to feel superior to someone, and, being a Russian, he could pretend that he was superior to the Poles. Pyotr shouldered his ax and followed Ivan down the ravine. Just beyond the mouth of the ravine, a dozen Polish carpenters were working furiously to complete the bridge before nightfall.

They'll do it, too, Pyotr thought gloomily.

He heard old Ivan shout at Urban, the Polish master carpenter, telling him to send four of his worthless rascals up the ravine to fetch the tree. He saw Urban's lips move as he gave a quiet order, and then four carpenters dropped their tools and hurried up the path that bordered the frozen creek.

"Sit down," old Ivan said. "Don't you have sense enough to rest when you get the chance?"

Pyotr sat down on one of the big logs that formed a square around the laborers' fire. He leaned toward the flame, extending his hands to warm them. Then a gust of wind blew smoke into his face and he turned away, coughing. Across the frozen creek, that fat toad Krusekopf and the other two German guards were squatting around a flat rock, playing cards, probably skat. They had propped their weapons—two rifles and a machine pistol—against the stump of a tree, and they paid no attention whatever to the Polish and Russian laborers whom they were supposed to be guarding. In fact, they were so intent on their game that they had allowed their own private fire to burn too low. There was nothing left but a heap of gray ash that gave off occasional wisps of smoke.

Just before it goes out, Pyotr thought, they'll yell for me to come over and start it up again. They can't be bothered to throw wood on their own fire, even when there's a pile of it two paces behind their backs. I cut that wood. For two days all I've done is cut wood and . . .

"Lad," old Ivan said, "if you don't stop gritting your teeth you'll lose them all before you're thirty."

"I've got a long way to go before I'm thirty," Pyotr said, but he stopped gritting his teeth. He reminded himself that old Ivan meant well. Old Ivan always meant well.

"It's just that I'm so tired of waiting," he said. "Why don't the Americans do something?"

"They'll do enough when they're ready," old Ivan said. "They're just not ready yet."

"They might have attacked," Pyotr said, "yesterday or today or any day now. If I could just find a way to stay west of the Rhine a day or so longer—"

"Sshhh," old Ivan said. "Here come the Poles."

Pyotr looked up the ravine. The four Poles were coming down the path, carrying the pine tree he and Ivan had felled. They walked briskly despite their heavy burden. It would be years before he could carry that much weight so easily.

"They certainly are strong," he said.

"Strong and dumb, like oxen," old Ivan said. "If they had any sense they could have made this bridge-building job last three days instead of two."

"The Germans wanted it built in two days," Pyotr said. "They do what the Germans want. And so do you. And so do I. In another hour or so the truck will come and we'll all pile in. Then they'll drive us back across the Rhine— and that will be the end of it."

Old Ivan dug into his coat pocket and pulled out his stubby pipe. He put the stem into his mouth and sucked on it. He hadn't had any tobacco for a week but he liked to suck his pipe, remembering what tobacco used to taste like. He watched the four Poles lay the tree across sawhorses. They measured the long log quickly, then set to work with saws. The sawing made enough noise for Ivan's purpose, and he turned his head toward Pyotr.

"Lad," he said, "if the Americans came all the way from the Channel to the Rhine in six months, what makes you think the river is going to stop them?"

"Well—"

"By spring they'll drive the Germans deep into Germany, and no matter how often the Germans move us to the rear, they'll reach us finally." Old Ivan chuckled, a husky rumble that was half amused, half grim. "Or maybe our own Russian troops will reach us first. It doesn't really matter. The point is, when the Germans run out of territory, they'll run out of labor camps, and then we'll be free."

Pyotr nodded dumbly. Old Ivan had explained it all so many times that Pyotr believed him—almost. Perhaps the Americans could cross the Rhine. They might even fight their way through the Siegfried Line. But it would take so long. Old Ivan could wait. He must be at least fifty, and it was easy to wait, to be patient, when you were that old. Pyotr had made many truck rides like the one he would make tonight, and always, at the end of each ride, there was the same miserable collection of unpainted wooden barracks with a high wire fence around it. The labor camp was his cage, and the cage was his world. He was fifteen years old, and he had lived the last three of those years in cages.

He swallowed because his throat was dry.

"I still say," he whispered hoarsely, "that if I get a chance I'll make a run for it."

"Fool," old Ivan said. "Crazy young fool."

Pyotr sat there wretchedly, watching the carpenters without really seeing them. The four Poles finished sawing the pine tree into usable lengths and went back under the bridge. He was dimly aware of hammering—and then a voice across the creek barked a single German word:

"Boy!"

"Yes, corporal." Pyotr sprang to his feet. He ran to the edge of the creek, slid halfway across the smooth ice, gathered himself, and slid once more. He bounded up the far bank, heading for the woodpile. The fat corporal named Krusekopf snarled, "Why did you let the fire die out? Where have you been hiding, you lousy Russian brat?" But by that time Pyotr had reached the woodpile. He made his hands dart about frantically, seeking good pieces of kindling. He made his whole body express mute apology, fear, a desperate desire to win forgiveness. He dropped the kindling and hunched over the charred logs of the dying fire, clearing away ashes. This done, he fanned the logs with his hat until they glowed red again. He stacked kindling against the logs, then went back to the pile for larger pieces of wood.

Krusekopf swore, grunted with disgust, and shuffled the cards for another hand of skat.

I fooled you, Pyotr thought. I didn't answer you and I got away with it. Oh, I've learned the tricks, you fat toad. I've learned all of them and I'll fool you every time.

It was a game he played, but there was little satisfaction in it, really. His tricks were such small, petty tricks, and in the end the Germans had a roaring fire for their comfort. They were the victors, always.

Pyotr slid back across the creek in two swooping glides. He would have liked to spend his last hour here just sliding, but if he tried it Krusekopf would notice him having fun and start bellowing again. Glumly he went back to the

laborers' fire and sat down beside Ivan. Ivan refused to
speak to him. He didn't know what to say or do to make
amends, and he felt lonely.

Silent minutes passed. Then, suddenly, Polish carpenters
began to come out from under the bridge. They dropped
their tools in a pile and sat down on the logs around the
fire. They stomped their feet and flapped their arms, warming up. Only the master carpenter, Urban, remained beneath the bridge, and he seemed to be just checking things,
rather than working.

"Are you through?" Pyotr asked in Polish.

"Through is right," said Mieroszewski, the youngest of
the lot. "All we have to do now is wait for the truck."

He's so cheerful, Pyotr thought. Well, he's eighteen and
an apprentice carpenter. That's a lot better than being fifteen and only fit for chopping down little trees and tending fires. I suppose it keeps him from feeling like a slave.
I wish . . .

Pyotr blinked. He had raised his head, still deep in
thought, and now he saw a line of men coming down the
road. The men wore gray uniforms, and all but the leader
were carrying boxes on their shoulders.

"Look," he said. "Look at what's coming down the road!"

Everybody looked. The line of German soldiers came
closer. They wore parkas instead of overcoats, and there
was something odd about their boots. Ordinary German
soldiers clumped along in leather jackboots, but these men
moved noiselessly in boots made of some softer material.

Felt boots, Pyotr thought, and a tingle of fear ran
through his body.

"Paratroopers," he said.

"Yes," old Ivan murmured, close beside him. "The wild
ones. The crazy ones."

Across the creek, the three guards got to their feet and
began to mutter among themselves. Urban came out from

under the bridge, saw the approaching paratroopers, and hurried toward the laborers' fire.

"Come back under the bridge and try to look busy," he said in a low voice.

The carpenters started toward the bridge.

"No, no!" Urban said. "Get your tools first!"

The Poles reached for their tools, but it was too late.

"Well, well!" came the hearty shout from the road. "Look at the reception committee all ready to greet us!"

Everybody stood stock still, watching the paratroopers approach the bridge. The leader was a sergeant-major—a *Feldwebel*. He grinned as he walked up to the edge of the bridge. He stopped. He turned around leisurely and said, "All right, lads, drop your boxes." His men obeyed literally, dropping their boxes heavily in the mud and snow. Then they formed a loose group behind the feldwebel. They were tall, lean, young and tough. Pyotr could see that, even as his mind registered the fact that with those hooded parkas half concealing their faces, they looked like military monks.

"You've done a quick job," the feldwebel said, addressing Corporal Krusekopf. "The Amis bombed out this bridge the day before yesterday, and here you've got it all rebuilt for us. Congratulations, corporal."

"Thank you," Krusekopf said uneasily. "We worked as fast as we could. . . ." His voice trailed off. He began again. "You see, the Army Engineers were busy. They had other work to do. And here were these foreign laborers lying around the camp, doing nothing. So it was decided—"

"We know all that," the feldwebel said. "Even a bunch of worthless foreigners can bridge a little creek on a back road. But you did a fine job, corporal. Just fine." White teeth flashed in the feldwebel's lean young face. It was not a pleasant smile. It would have done credit to a hungry wolf. "We're in luck," the feldwebel said.

"Luck?" Krusekopf repeated blankly.

"Yes, indeed." The feldwebel chuckled. "Here we are with fifteen boxes of rations—and there you are with fifteen men to carry them for us!"

There was a long silence. Pyotr held his breath.

"But—but these men are through work for the day," Corporal Krusekopf said. "Their camp is ten kilometers east of the Rhine, and they have to go back by truck. The truck will be here in an hour—"

"The truck can wait," the feldwebel said. "We need them to carry these ration boxes."

"But I have orders—"

The feldwebel bounded down the slope in half a dozen lithe strides. He rammed the muzzle of his Schmeisser pistol hard into Krusekopf's belly. Krusekopf's breath burst from him with an audible whoosh.

"Do you know what you're looking at, fat man?"

"Why, yes," Krusekopf gasped. "You're—"

"Paratroops! Elite troops. The best shock troops in the world. That's what we are!"

Krusekopf nodded jerkily.

"They're supposed to hold us in reserve, fat man. They're supposed to train us for parachute jumps, special assaults. But do they do that?"

Krusekopf shook his head. "I suppose they've run out of planes to carry you," he said apologetically.

"Sure, they've run out of planes. So they stick us in the line like ordinary infantry. They leave us there for months. They even make us hand-carry our rations—" The feldwebel cursed, raging insanely. "We're tired of it, fat man. Do you hear me? Tired of it!"

Krusekopf licked his lips. "Naturally," he said. "You should be treated better—"

"Shut up! Shut up and listen. Our position is just a few kilometers from here. These Polish swine can make the trip in an hour, and in another hour they'll be back here. All you have to do is leave one guard behind to meet the truck. He tells the driver to wait, and he waits. Then you all pile into the truck and go back to where it's safe and peaceful. What could be simpler, fat man?"

Krusekopf looked at his fellow guards. They returned his gaze helplessly. Krusekopf sighed.

"Schwartz," he said huskily, "you stay behind and wait for the truck. Tell the driver . . ." His thick, middle-aged body sagged. "You know what to tell him, Schwartz."

Schwartz nodded. Krusekopf and Globke, the other guard, went over to the tree stump and picked up their weapons.

"All right," Krusekopf said, "you men go up to the road and pick up those ration boxes."

For a moment, the Poles just stood there. Then Urban said softly, in Polish, "Let's go." They plodded up the slope. Minutes later the column began to march, paratroopers on one side of the road, laborers in single file on the other, with Corporal Krusekopf in the lead and Globke guarding the rear. The pace was slow, because nobody was in a hurry to reach the front lines.

Nobody but a fifteen-year-old Russian boy named Pyotr.

Chapter 2

BARRAGE!

The ration box had been heavy to lift in the first place, but now, after a march of almost two kilometers, it seemed to weigh a ton. Pyotr shifted the box from his aching left shoulder to his right shoulder, but his right shoulder was already sore from a previous stretch of carrying. His feet dragged. He tripped over a rock and almost fell. He staggered on.

"This is what you wanted," old Ivan said behind him. "I hope you're satisfied."

Pyotr didn't have breath enough to answer. He hoped he wouldn't fall down, and at the same time he wished he would fall and get it over with. He shook his head and blinked to clear the sweat from his eyes—sweat was pouring from him in temperature below zero. He took another step, slipped on slick ice, and fell sprawling. Old Ivan stumbled over him, tried to regain his balance, and came down with a crash. Then the man behind Ivan piled onto the heap, and the paratroopers roared with laughter.

"Looks like the kid's through for a while," the feldwebel said cheerfully. "All right, you men, take a break."

Pyotr heard ration boxes thump on the road. He lay across his own box, which somehow had fallen under him, until Ivan reached up, caught hold of his sleeve, and pulled him into the ditch. He gasped, "Thank you, Ivan," and lay with the side of his head half buried in snow. For five minutes he didn't move, but then, strangely, the ground began to throb beneath his ear. The throbbing became a steady, heavy thumping noise. He raised his head. In the gathering dusk, he saw the battered remains of what had once been a village. Houses were tumbled heaps of wood and stone. The only building in the village which had not been completely wrecked was the church—and of the church, only the spire remained, pointing into the darkening sky like a broken finger.

Beyond the spire, Pyotr saw a flickering reddish glow. Shellfire. Somewhere along the rim of the Colmar Pocket, big guns were hard at work, destroying yet another village.

"Feldwebel," Corporal Krusekopf said, "is that our artillery or theirs?"

"I don't know," the feldwebel said. "Probably it's theirs, though. The Amis are always shelling at night. They never leave well enough alone."

The rumbling of guns continued. The red glow increased.

"It's the Amis," the feldwebel decided finally. "They're pounding our line over near Katzenthal."

"Are we going anywhere near Katzenthal?" Krusekopf asked.

"No." The feldwebel stood up. "But we'd better be on our way. They might decide to shell Turckheim for a change —and that's where we *are* going."

. "On your feet!" Krusekopf shouted. "Everybody on your—"

"Shut up!" the feldwebel said. "I'm in command here." He muttered something about fat Volksturm corporals, and then he bellowed, "On your feet! Get moving, you worthless scum!"

Pyotr lifted his box waist-high, gave a desperate heave, and managed to catch it on his shoulder. He groaned as the weight bore down on him, but when the column began to march he marched too. Through the village streets they went, two straggling lines of men surrounded by utter deso-

lation. The ghost town dwindled into smaller piles of rubble, and then it ceased to exist, except in memory. The
column crossed a wide expanse of snowy fields. The road
began to climb into the hills. Pyotr barely reached the top
of the first hill, but after that he felt nothing and cared
about nothing. He plodded numbly over a second hill, a
third, a fourth. Each hill was higher than the last, but it
didn't matter any more.

The road dipped into a valley. Parallel snowdrifts to the
right and left showed the location of vineyards where, in
summertime, Alsatian farmers tended the grapes that made
Moselle wine famous throughout the world. A sizeable town
occupied the floor of the valley, and most of the houses were
still standing. At the edge of town, soldiers stepped from behind a stone wall and challenged the column. The feldwebel
gave the password and the column went on. The houses
were all blacked out, but the streets were not silent. Pyotr
heard German voices from time to time, so he knew that this
town was held by the Wehrmacht. He was near the front
lines now. In fact, this town might be a front-line strongpoint. He dragged his leaden feet, following the man ahead
of him. The last house fell behind. And then he heard the
wailing in the air.

"Hit the dirt!" the feldwebel yelled.

The faint wails grew into screams. The screaming came
closer. The paratroopers disappeared as if by magic from
the left side of the road. On the right side, the Poles
dropped their boxes and tried to hide behind them. The
screaming increased, blended into one continuous deafen-
ing howl. "Down, boy! Down!" old Ivan shouted, and Pyotr
dropped flat in the ditch.

The first shell exploded. The ground seemed to lurch,
slamming its icy hardness against his chest and the side of
his face. The blow knocked the wind out of him. He tried
to protect his face by raising his head, but when the sec-

ond shell landed this only resulted in a harder slam against the ground. The third and fourth shells landed, and each time it felt like the blow of a club.

Then there was silence.

"Lad," old Ivan said.

Pyotr licked his lips. He tasted blood.

"Pyotr, are you all right?"

"Yes, Ivan."

"Lie still, lad. There may be more."

The wailing began again with Ivan's last word. Pyotr shuddered. I can't stand it, he thought, and looked around wildly. At first he saw only the prostrate bodies of men cowering behind ration boxes. Then, in a flash, he understood why the paratroopers had all run off to the left.

"Ivan!" he shouted. "Get off the road!"

He couldn't even hear his own voice as he flung himself to the right. Scrambling desperately, he cleared the hump of packed earth beside the ditch, and then he was falling, falling. The screaming in the air ended in four gigantic explosions, but now he was rolling in deep snow, and the snow cushioned the impact. He lay panting on his back, almost buried in snow, and he wondered if Ivan had left the road also.

It was impossible to tell. Four more shells came over, but now they were landing in the town itself, at least a hundred meters away. Pyotr raised his head and tried to get his bearings. Another flight of shells screeched overhead, and then he understood everything.

The road ran along a low embankment. It was a few feet higher than the fields on either side. The paratroopers had all dived into the field to the left because the shells were coming from the right, and the embankment offered some protection. Pyotr, lying at the bottom of the right side of the embankment, was less safe than the paratroopers, but far better off than the Poles who were still hugging the ditch beside the road itself. And poor old Ivan . . .

Pyotr called Ivan's name, but there was no answer. He forced himself to be calm, even when he heard that terrible wailing begin again. The American artillery seemed to be concentrating on the town now, instead of the road, but he should find a safer place than this. His eyes searched the field. It was nothing but a flat expanse of snow and stubble. He scanned the embankment and saw what looked like a black hole only a few meters away. He waited until the shells exploded in the town, and then he made a dash for the hole.

It was the opening of a drain pipe that ran all the way through the embankment. And it was large enough. Barely large enough. He slid in feet first, and kept pushing himself farther in until not even his head was visible from outside. He waited, shivering in the dank, icy-bottomed pipe. Shells kept on bursting for what seemed to be a long time, but finally the barrage ended.

Up on the road, someone was shouting. The voice echoed hollowly in the pipe, but he could make out words. The feldwebel was ordering everybody to stand up, to form a column again, to get moving.

Now was the time to leave the pipe. It was safe enough. But . . .

They can't see me, Pyotr thought.

"—then where is he?" the voice of the feldwebel said, directly overhead. "How could he vanish in thin air?"

"I don't know," old Ivan's voice said faintly. "He was lying in the ditch right in front of me, and then—"

"Here's a path in the snow," Corporal Krusekopf's voice broke in. "Maybe he ran to that barn over there."

"The barn's too far," the feldwebel objected. "He's hiding around here somewhere. But where?"

"I told you I don't know." Old Ivan sounded desperate.

He began calling, "Pyotr! Pyotr! Where are you, Pyotr?"

I'm here, Pyotr called back silently. I know I should come out, Ivan, but I can't. I'm frightened half to death but I've got to stay hidden. I've got to escape from them and this is the only way. . . .

"The devil with him," the feldwebel said angrily. "Let him go. Let him get lost between the lines for all I care. The crazy kid—"

"But maybe he's wounded," old Ivan said. "Maybe—"

"Maybe he's dead," the feldwebel finished brutally. "Go pick up your box and get in line."

Pyotr rested the side of his head against the ice in the bottom of the pipe. His head felt hot. He was dizzy with tension, and the ice seemed to calm him. He heard the feldwebel tell Schwartz, the guard, to pick up the crazy kid's box and carry it. Then he heard shuffling noises, and a last, faint, "Pyotr! Answer me, boy!" from Ivan, far down the road now, and then he heard nothing.

Nothing.

Pyotr raised his head. He ran his tongue along the inside of his cheek, where he had bitten himself. He had stopped bleeding. And now he must leave this hole.

He couldn't move.

Get out, he told himself. *You've got to get out now.*

He hooked his fingers over the rim of the concrete pipe. With a single, convulsive movement, he flung himself all the way out of the pipe. He lay still for a moment in the snow, and then he stood up. The road was empty. Dimly, in the weak moonlight, he saw the path Krusekopf had mentioned. He had rolled directly down the path at the point where it left the road, and that was the reason they hadn't been able to trace him through the snow. The path wandered across the field. He squinted. Was that a thatched roof over there? Yes, a long, wide thatched roof. Judging from size alone, it had to be a barn roof. He glanced over

his shoulder. He couldn't see the nearest house from here, so probably he couldn't be seen either. He would have to risk it.

He started walking. Instinctively, he bent double, and soon he was running. Now he could see the barn itself—a large whitewashed structure, almost as white as the snow of the fields that surrounded it. He ran faster. He reached the wall of the barn, then rounded the corner. There was the door. He crept toward it, hugging the wall. The door was half open. He heard no sound. An icy wind swept across the field and whispered wickedly in his ear. He shivered. He couldn't stay outside any longer. He would freeze.

Pyotr slipped through the narrow opening. He listened. He went farther in, veering to the right, waving his hand from side to side in the pitch blackness. After a moment his hand struck wood. He advanced three steps and struck wood again.

Empty stalls, he thought. I can sleep here.

His whole body relaxed with the thought—and in that instant a terrible bellow rent the air. He stiffened, every muscle rigid. The savage bellow came again, but this time it sounded oddly familiar. Pyotr held his head in his trembling hands, trying to make his mind work. It sounded like . . .

The next time the cow mooed, Pyotr leaned limply against the side of the stall, giggling helplessly. He had been scared out of his wits by one of the gentlest animals living. Thank heaven she was living!

He groped his way back to the door. He swung the door shut, put his back against it, and unbuttoned his old, threadbare civilian workman's short coat. He fished in his jacket pocket and pulled out a box of matches. Cupping his hands, he lighted a match.

The glow revealed a bucket standing just inside the door. He scooped up a handful of straw, threw it into the bucket, and dropped the match into the straw. The resulting fire told him all he needed to know. The small windows, set high in the wall, had been blacked out with heavy wooden shutters. The door fitted tightly. He couldn't see any sign of a lock or bar for the door, but at least his presence would not be betrayed by light. He stifled another fit of giggling, then pulled the stub of a candle out of his pocket. There had been no electricity in the labor camp barracks, and like everyone else he hoarded candles. He lighted the candle and walked down the wide aisle. The cow wasn't in a stall. She was standing in the aisle, looking straight at him.

Pyotr approached the cow cautiously. She was a large black-and-brown creature, without horns, and her brown eyes were soft, as a cow's eyes should be. He put a hand on her head, scratching gently, and she raised her muzzle, trying earnestly to kiss him. He avoided the wet caress and walked around her side. She was miserably thin—her hip bones jutted out like the ends of an inverted coat hanger— but her milk bag was full.

For a moment he debated her nationality. Alsace being a border province, she could be either French or German. But she was such a nice cow. He decided she was French.

"Come, Yvette," he said. "Step into this stall, *ma chérie*."

But Yvette had a will of her own. After nearly five minutes of pushing and coaxing, she was still standing in the aisle, mooing plaintively.

I'm hungry, she seemed to be saying. So hungry.

Pyotr picked up the candle and went exploring. In the rear of the barn he found rows of milk cans, pails, and milking stools. Pitchforks, too. Fearing the worst, he climbed the ladder to the loft. To his surprise, he saw that a considerable pile of hay remained. He pitched some down to the concrete floor and then hauled it in a wheelbarrow up the aisle to a clean stall. He piled the hay in a manger—and suddenly there was Yvette, in the stall with him, munching vigorously.

Pyotr left the stall. He waited awhile, then returned with a pail and milking stool. He had milked a cow just once in his life, when his father had taken him on a visit to a farm near Kiev. The trick was to close your hand gradually around the teat, squeezing one finger at a time, rhythmically. He tried it. Yvette glanced over her shoulder. Then she whisked her tail and slapped Pyotr in the face. Pyotr winced and tried again. It took him ten minutes to draw the first squirt, and during that time Yvette had slapped him again with her tail, stepped on his foot, and leaned against him, almost crushing him between her bony ribs and the wooden wall of the stall.

Patience, Pyotr told himself, and went on trying.

An hour later, perspiring, tail-lashed and bruised, he had a quarter of a pail of warm milk, fresh from the udder. Yvette had stopped eating. She was just staring blankly at the wall before her, so Pyotr began to drink the milk. He didn't bother to look for a dipper. He tilted the pail and drank.

With most of the milk inside of him, he felt better. He hooked his fingers around the string which circled his neck, and pulled his father's watch from its hiding place beneath his shirt. The golden hands told him that it was almost nine o'clock. He didn't want to waste candles. He only had two short ones. It was time for him to go to sleep.

Or try to.

He piled straw on the floor of the stall next to Yvette's and lay down on it. His body was stiff, sore, strained and trembling with fatigue. He couldn't make himself sleep. Time ticked by, and still he lay awake.

Then he heard noises in Yvette's stall. He got up and went around the partition. He waved his hand in the air but failed to locate Yvette. He bent down, and then his hand touched a hairy hide. Yvette was lying down.

"Yvette," he said politely, "do you mind if I join you?"

Yvette mooed softly.

Minutes later Pyotr lay snuggled against a huge, warm body. Yvette didn't move. Soon he, too, ceased to move. He slept.

When he awoke, he awoke all at once, every sense alert. He listened. He could hear the far-off ripple of machine-gun fire, the muffled thump of mortars, the plop-plop of rifles. The sound of battle was continuous, raging in a wide arc. Quietly he got up and lighted his stub of candle. He pulled out his father's watch. It was one minute after eleven, and this was the night of February 1, 1945. He dropped the watch back inside his shirt and stood motionless, listening to the gathering storm of fire. This was it—the attack he had been waiting for, praying for.

In the middle of the night, the French and Americans had launched their big drive to wipe out the Colmar Pocket. Now the Germans would fight desperately to hold their last bridgehead west of the Rhine. But they would fail. They must fail, so he could be free of them forever.

All he had to do was wait. And stay alive.

Chapter 3

GHOSTS IN THE NIGHT

Just before dawn, Pyotr made a quick, shivering dash outside to fill two buckets with snow. Yvette licked both buckets dry, and then she allowed him to milk her. His nervous stomach would not hold much milk, so he poured most of it down the drain in the center of the aisle. The milk steamed in the cold air and left a ring of foam around the drain. Pyotr felt guilty about the waste, but he comforted himself with the thought that he could milk Yvette again later in the day. For an hour he just paced the aisle, filling in time.

Then, with the first light of day, the bombardment began.

All morning long, and far into the afternoon, flights of shells screamed over the ridge to the north. They burst in a merciless, regular pattern, shattering the houses in the north end of town, marching in precise lines until they reached the last houses to the south, then starting over again, caving in roofs, toppling walls, systematically destroying every building in their path.

Pyotr saw it all.

Very early in the morning, he had rebelled at being shut up in this dark barn, unable to tell what was going on. He explored the tool room, found two stepladders, and set the taller one up under a window in the north wall. Luckily the shutter latched on the inside, so he propped it open and peered out. All he saw was the ridge over which the shells were coming, and the ridge looked quite bare, except for the tiers of snowdrifts which marked the vineyards. He closed the window, carried the ladder to the south wall, and set it up under another window. This time he saw the town, and the bombardment. Hundreds of meters of snowy field lay between this barn and the doomed town. He could not be safer here—nor could he have a clearer view.

He watched in fascinated horror, hour after hour.

Several times during the morning he saw German soldiers. This astonished him, for he could not understand how anybody stayed alive in that barrage. But apparently they did. After all, the shells were wrecking only the roofs and upper stories of the houses, and the Germans could hide in the cellars. Every time he saw the Germans, they were either carrying stretchers into a large, roofless house near the center of town, or running to or from a smaller, less badly damaged house directly across the street. He decided that the first house must be a front-line hospital, and the other a headquarters of some sort.

Once, during a brief lull in the bombardment, three ambulances came careening down the main street. They stopped at the hospital, received loads of wounded, and dashed out of town again. They did not return.

Late in the afternoon, Pyotr became so weary that he had to forsake his vigil on the stepladder. He lowered himself into the pile of straw in the stall next to Yvette's and tried to relax. He knew he couldn't sleep, but he must rest. He closed his burning eyes, then opened them again. The shelling had stopped. Why?

He sprang up. He climbed the stepladder so fast that he almost upset it. He looked out the window. The town seemed deserted. Then he saw them—German soldiers pouring out of the houses, moving toward the north end of town. He listened. He heard far-off German voices shouting orders, but no firing of any kind. He watched the Germans run through the streets, all heading north.

The attack would come from the north. . . .

Pyotr leaped to the floor, picked up the ladder, and lunged toward the north wall. He tripped, fell headlong, bringing the ladder down with a crash. Yvette mooed fretfully—she, who had been quiet throughout the bombardment. He got up again, righted the ladder, and swarmed up the rungs like a monkey. He propped open the shutter. As if he had given a signal, machine guns and rifles went off with a crackling roar.

A swarm of tiny figures came over the ridge.

The Americans!

He didn't doubt for a second that they were Americans. The French First Army, which was supposed to play the major role in the Colmar area, had never seemed quite real to him. He had thought of the Americans as his saviors ever since their landings in Normandy and the south of France, so these must be Americans.

Some of the little figures dropped flat on top of the ridge. They clustered in twos and threes, and he could tell that they were firing machine guns, and perhaps other weapons, at the Germans down in the town. The others advanced in small groups of about a dozen men each, with a good deal of space between men. Some of the small figures tumbled in the snow, and his stomach clenched in a spasm of anxiety. Then he took hope again. After all, not many men were falling. Scattered out that way, they offered poor targets for the German machine guns. The little groups—squads, he supposed—raced down the hill toward the first row of snow-drifts.

Now they must get through the vineyards.

He expected the Americans to trample through or leap over the racks of grapevines, but they stopped and fell flat. One group crawled through the snow to a snowdrift, and suddenly the snowdrift exploded. Pyotr saw a great shower of snow and earth, followed by a muffled boom. Now several of the little figures were lying twisted on the ground, and the others stayed where they were, almost hidden in the snow.

Another squad crawled toward a snowdrift. They moved cautiously, clearing away the snow ahead of them as they advanced. They reached the snowdrift. They began burrowing into it, groping forward inches at a time, so that he could scarcely see them move at all.

Oh, why didn't they hurry?

The answer came before the question was fully formed. Another explosion shook the side of the hill, flinging the little figures of the Americans about like toys. The Germans had mined or booby-trapped the vineyards!

And the Americans couldn't advance at all.

Hopelessly, fighting a rising tide of sickness in his stomach, Pyotr watched the Americans retreat. They gathered their wounded and dragged them toward the top of the ridge, while the machine gunners and riflemen fired furiously to keep the Germans in the town from raising their heads. But even though the German machine gun and rifle fire slackened, their mortars, concealed far to the rear, could go to work without fear. Mushrooms of snow and dirt rose all over the crest of the hill, and more Americans had to be led, carried, or dragged to safety. It took a long time for the Americans to effect their escape from that mortar barrage. They lost heavily before they all disappeared beyond the ridge.

Finally the last of them were gone. The attack had failed —and night was closing in.

Pyotr sat on top of the stepladder for a long time. The machine guns ceased to chatter. Even the mortars fell silent. Darkness surrounded him in the barn, and outside there was no moon. Beaten, motionless, he sat there in a pitch-black world that even God seemed to have forgotten.

Yvette mooed. He ought to milk her. He ought to fill his

stomach to stop the steady ache of emptiness. But he didn't
care. It was too much trouble to move.

Yvette mooed again.

Her milk bag must be full, he thought. Maybe it hurts.
All right, I'll milk her.

The soreness of his muscles almost made him cry out as
he climbed down the ladder. He pulled one of the candles
out of his pocket, lighted it, and approached Yvette's stall.
Yvette mooed again. Then, outside the barn door, a German voice said, "Hear that? I told you they left a cow behind!"

Pyotr blew out the candle. He ran sure-footedly down
the aisle. He reached the tool room just as the door opened.
He flattened himself against the wall, breathing hard. A yel-
low ray darted through a crack between boards, then went
on, searching. They had a flashlight out there.

"You see, it was a big herd," the same German voice said.
"Twenty stalls, twenty dairy cows. Captain Nolte ordered
the herd to be shipped east of the Rhine, but he said
leave one behind for the French family that owned them.
What became of the French family I don't know, but there's
the cow they left behind. Big beast, isn't she?"

"And thin," another voice said. "*Himmel*, is she skinny!"

The Germans sounded as if they had been drinking. It
was not surprising, considering their victory, and the fact
that almost every house in Alsace seemed to have a barrel
of Moselle wine ripening in its cellar.

"Ever milked a cow, Karl?"

"No, Helmut. I'm from Hamburg."

"And I'm from Munich. Just a couple of city boys, eh?"

Both Germans laughed. Then they began to argue as to
who should do the milking, and who was to hold the flashlight. They finally agreed, and Pyotr heard the milk pail
rattle. There was a moment of silence. Yvette mooed. Helmut cursed angrily.

"Hold her tail!" he shouted.

Karl laughed long and loud.

"I said hold her tail! She's slapping me in the face with it!" There was more laughter, more cursing. "Never mind her tail!" Helmut roared. "Push her away from me! She's leaning against me! She's crushing me—"

Pyotr heard Yvette's hoof strike the pail. The pail clanged on the concrete floor. It began to roll. Helmut swore louder.

"Why don't you give up?" Karl said, still laughing. "We don't have to have milk, you know. Let's go back to town and drink some more wine."

"All right," Helmut growled. "All right. But I did want a little milk for a change." He cursed once more, and Pyotr heard a thud. Yvette mooed again, loudly. Helmut had kicked her!

There was another thud, Helmut screamed. That meant Yvette had kicked *him!*

"No, Helmut," Karl said. "Don't do it. Remember, she's only a cow. She—"

The rifle sounded like a cannon in the enclosed space of the barn. Yvette bawled once, piteously, and then there was no sound at all.

"You didn't have to do that," Karl said at last. "It's bad enough as it is, without killing cows—"

"She almost broke my leg," Helmut snarled. "What did you expect me to do when she kicked me in the leg?"

"Never mind," Karl said. "Let's go drink some more wine."

Heavy footsteps clumped toward the door. Pyotr waited for about five minutes, then left the tool room. He walked quietly, surely, up the aisle; by this time he knew exactly where everything was in the barn, without the aid of light. He turned into Yvette's stall, bent down, put out his hand. Yvette was dead. He could tell that just by touching her.

He backed out of the stall. He sat down in the aisle and

lowered his face into his hands. After a while he began to cry.

"Just a cow," he sobbed. "Just a skinny old cow."

But saying it didn't help. He sat there crying hopelessly. He cried until his insides hurt, and there were no more tears in him. Then he raised his head.

The door was open. Even though this was a moonless night, the sky outside looked lighter than the interior of the barn, and he could see snow on the ground.

He ought to close the door and light a candle.

No, he didn't want to light a candle. If he did that, he would have to look at Yvette.

Well, at least he should close the door.

He made himself get up. He started for the door. But now, for some reason, the snow on the ground was moving.

Snow—moving?

He stopped dead in his tracks.

The snow only seemed to be moving, because many dark legs were walking over its whiteness. And now the lower half of the sky looked black because many men had gathered in the doorway, blotting out the pale light. He could hear their feet shuffling on concrete. They were coming down the aisle, coming toward him!

"Kamerad!" he croaked. *"Nicht schiessen!"*

He stepped forward, praying that they would not shoot.

"Halt!" a hard voice said.

Pyotr halted. He heard dozens of boots pounding on the concrete as the soldiers hastily left the doorway and scattered in the barn. The door closed with a bang. Now the barn was pitch-black. Suddenly a ray of light lanced out of the dark. It struck his eyes. He blinked.

"It's a kid!" someone said. "A French civilian kid!"

Pyotr almost fainted with relief. He moistened his lips. He managed to speak.

"Not French," he said. "Russian. And I am very glad to meet you, gentlemen from America!"

Chapter 4

THE THIRD PLATOON

"Well, what do you know?" a voice from one of the stalls said. "He speaks perfect English."

"Sounds like a limey to me," another voice said. "What's a Russian kid doing with a British accent?"

"All European schools teach English with a British accent," a third, quiet voice said. "It sounds more formal than any of our American accents, so—"

"Wait a minute," said the hard voice behind the flashlight. "Let's check for blackout before we talk about this kid."

"The barn is completely blacked out," Pyotr said. "All of the windows have shutters and the door fits snugly."

"Hmmm. All right, you men, light candles."

The mellow glow of candles spread over the front half of the barn. There must be thirty men here, Pyotr thought. Maybe more. They all wore green, hip-length jackets and olive-drab trousers tucked into laced leather boots. Above the visor of each helmet, a red emblem stood out clearly.

And their faces . . .

Timid but eager, he looked at the Americans themselves, instead of their uniforms. They were tired, drawn, grim and unshaven—but they didn't look cruel, like the German paratroopers. They seemed to be just average young men, hardened by battle. Some of them looked like Russians. Two wore glasses. Strange, he mused. I expected them to be huge, but they come in all shapes and sizes, like everyone else.

Then he gulped.

Directly in front of him stood a wide-shouldered giant who carried a short rifle in one hand and a flashlight in the other. The giant had a jutting jaw and piercing gray eyes. He smiled thinly and said:

"Okay, Russky, what are you doing here?"

As briefly as he could, Pyotr told his story. The giant nodded from time to time, and asked occasional questions. When Pyotr finished his eyes looked almost friendly.

"That took guts," he said.

"Guts?" Pyotr said.

"That's American for courage," the giant said.

"I didn't feel very courageous," Pyotr said. "I just did what I had to do, that's all."

"That's all anybody can do, Russky."

Pyotr smiled. The giant smiled back. In fact, he grinned.

"May I ask what *you* are doing here?" Pyotr said.

The giant frowned thoughtfully. Then he shrugged.

"I don't suppose it matters," he said. "We're the third platoon of Oboe Company—that's the outfit that tried to come over the ridge this afternoon. The CO sent us around to flank the krauts, but before we could move into position the company got hung up on the wire in the vineyards. You saw the booby traps going off yourself, so you know what happened. Anyway, we could have gone back to the company, but I decided we'd better stick around till tomorrow morning. It got cold in the woods out back, so I thought I'd take a chance and bring the platoon over to this barn. We figure to hole up here till just before dawn."

"And then you will attack the Germans?"

"Yep. We'll hit 'em in the flank, like I said."

"But what about—ah—I think you called it Oboe Company? Are you sure they will attack again?"

"Dead sure. It takes more than wire and mines to stop

Oboe Company. I'll bet Captain Croft has patrols out right now, cutting wire."

"I see," Pyotr said admiringly. How much confidence this man had in what he called his "outfit"!

A tall, thin soldier had edged close to Pyotr. He wore round, steel-rimmed glasses which made him look like an owl.

"What's your real name, Russky?"

"Pyotr Dmitrievich Pribylov," Pyotr said.

"Wow!" the giant said. "I guess we'll stick to Russky."

"But Pyotr means Peter," the thin soldier said. "We can call him Pete."

"Pete, huh? Well, that's better." The giant slung his carbine over his shoulder and put out a huge hand. "Howdy, Pete. I'm Wayne Cotton."

"How do you do, Mr. Cotton."

"We call him Bull," the thin soldier said, "and he's a tech sergeant, even though he doesn't wear any stripes. He runs this platoon with an iron hand."

"I can well believe it," Pyotr said, nursing his fingers. "And what is your name, sir?"

"Irving Lindner."

The giant laughed. The thin soldier raised his shoulders to almost ear level and sighed sadly.

"All right," he said, "Forget you ever heard the name Irving Lindner. Just call me Professor."

Pyotr nodded. He recognized the voice now. Irving Lindner was the one who had explained that all European schools taught English with a British accent. But he looked much too young to be a professor.

"I see you're puzzled," Irving Lindner said. "It's quite simple, really. I'm not a member of this platoon. I'm from the battalion intelligence section. I used to teach school in New York City and I read books and I wear glasses that

make me look like an owl. So they call me the Professor."
He grinned.

Pyotr grinned in return. He liked the Professor.

"I'm sure the title is a compliment," he said.

His words were drowned out by the barking baritone of
Bull Cotton, who said he wanted to "get things squared
away" for the night. Cotton ordered the first and second
squads to occupy the north stalls, and the third and fourth
squads to take the south stalls. He "posted security" by
sending four men out to "stand guard but keep out of
sight," and named other men to relieve the guards at two-
hour intervals.

"And you men over there," he snapped. "Go up in the
loft and start pitching down hay. We may as well sleep
soft tonight, because we sure won't be sleeping long."

Within fifteen minutes, the entire platoon had bedded
down on piles of hay. Pyotr found himself in a stall with
Sergeant Cotton, the Professor, and a short, thick-set runner, or messenger, named Bud Parente. Bull Cotton
stretched out on the hay and promptly began to snore. But
Bud said he was hungry and the Professor wanted to talk.

"Pete," the Professor said, "what did you do in that labor
camp? I mean, building that bridge must have been an
emergency project, wasn't it?"

"Yes, it was," Pyotr said, watching Bud tear open a waxed
cardboard box and tumble its contents into his lap. He saw
a packet of bisquits, a can of potted meat, a bar of choco-
late, a packet of powdered coffee, four cigarettes, and a
small roll of toilet paper. "During the cold months we either
cut wood or worked on the railroad, repairing bomb dam-
age," he went on absently. "During the summer we worked
as farm laborers."

"I see." The Professor adjusted his glasses on his long
nose. "But why did they put a boy in a slave labor camp?"

"They sent my father there. I went with him."

"Oh. Your father was a farmer?"

"My father was a doctor," Pyotr said. "He's dead."

The Professor grunted, then fell silent. Bud began opening the can of potted meat with a metal key. The key unwound a ribbon of steel from around the top of the can, but Bud stopped unwinding while a bit of ribbon was still attached to the can. Out of his pocket he drew several pyramid-shaped white pills. After sweeping some hay aside, he put the pills on the floor and struck a match. The little pyramids sent up low flames but no smoke.

"Heat pills," Bud said, noticing Pyotr's interest. "I took 'em off a dead kraut burp gunner day before yesterday. They work like American canned heat, only better."

"I've seen the Germans use them often," Pyotr said.

Bud picked up the metal key and the ribbon of steel allowed the can of potted meat to dangle over the fire. He looked up at Pyotr and grinned.

"It'll be hot in a couple of minutes," he said, and then stopped grinning. "Hey, kid, you hungry?"

"I—ah—drank some milk a while ago."

"How long ago?"

"Well—early this morning."

"Golly, why didn't you *say* so?" Bud pulled another box out of his jacket pocket. "This here's a lunch ration—"

"Wait a minute," the Professor said. "I've got two breakfast rations. Maybe he'd rather have hot coffee and eggs than cold lemonade and cheese. How about it, Pete?"

Pyotr nodded gratefully. Soon he was wolfing down bacon and eggs, and sipping coffee from the canteen cup the Professor had lent him. He sank his teeth into the fruit bar which also was part of the menu, and sighed.

"I must say the American Army eats well, gentlemen."

"That's just a K ration," Bud said, amused. "They're what we carry when we go into the attack. Wait till the company kitchen catches up with us. Then you'll see some real chow."

Pyotr offered the four cigarettes to Bud and the Professor. They divided the cigarettes, and as the Professor lighted one he eyed Pyotr like a kindly owl. Pyotr sensed that he wanted to ask more questions. Maybe that was his job, since he was a member of the intelligence section.

"About my father and me," he said. "We lived in Kiev. When the Germans captured the city, they sent people like my father wherever they thought their skills would be most useful to Germany. They needed a doctor for a big labor camp in Poland, so we went there—"

"We? You mean your whole family?"

"No, just my father and I." Pyotr hesitated. He didn't want to mention his two brothers or his sister, so he said, "My mother died when I was quite young, you see."

The Professor clucked sympathetically.

"After two years in the Polish camp, my father was sent here, to the Rhineland. He was the only doctor available for several camps. He worked too hard, traveling from camp to camp in an open truck in all kinds of weather. Last winter he contracted pneumonia and died—without a doctor." Pyotr stopped talking, but he could feel the Professor looking at him, so he had to finish. "I was thirteen," he said, "big enough to go out and work with the labor gangs. I've been working for a long time, Professor, and I'm tired. Not tired of working, but—" He wondered how he could explain to anyone who had always been free what it was like to live in a cage. No, he could not explain. "I was tired," he said, "so I escaped."

There was a long silence. The Professor cleared his throat.

"And you learned to speak English in school?" he said.

"Well, I started learning it in school. I didn't get very far. But in the Polish camp there was a professor who could speak several languages fluently—"

"A professor in a slave labor camp?"

"Yes. The camps were full of professional men whom the Germans didn't approve of. Doctors, teachers, lawyers. All kinds."

"Uh-huh. Tell me, Pete, when were you born, and where?"

"In 1929. In Kiev, the Ukraine, Russia."

"Russia," the Professor repeated. "Not the Union of Soviet Socialist Republics?"

Pyotr suspected a trap. Perhaps the Professor approved of the Soviet Union. On the other hand, perhaps not. He must take his chances. This was the time to speak out.

"My father used to say," he said slowly, "that the Soviet Union would last as long as the Communist Party lasted—but that Mother Russia would live forever."

"Your father didn't like the Communist Party?"

"He hated it."

"And your mother. Did she hate it too?"

"As I said, my mother died when I was very young—five, I think. I don't remember much about her, except that she was nice—" Pyotr leaned against the side of the stall. He was so tired now.

"Did you have any brothers or sisters, Pete?"

"Two brothers and one sister," Pyotr said wearily. "Both of my brothers were conscripted into the Red Army in 1941. Grigory was reported missing that year. Mitya was killed in action at Stalingrad in 1943—" Suddenly Pyotr felt dizzy. He lowered his head to his knees to keep from fainting. He didn't faint, but the memories, the bittersweet memories began coming back to haunt him. . . .

"Pete," the Professor said, "you don't have to answer these questions now. You can wait till you meet the intelligence officer. I just thought—"

"I understand," Pyotr murmured. "You're my friend. It will be easier if I tell you first." He made himself go on talking. "You see, my whole family is dead, except my sister. And she is lost."

"How do you mean, lost, Pete?"

"She married a Communist Party official. She hated us for not changing. She stopped coming to visit us. She was lost, my father said."

"I see, Pete. Take a rest now, until you feel better."

Pyotr nodded, as best he could with his head hanging between his knees. Sometimes he grieved for his father, sometimes for Grigory or Mitya. But always he missed Anna. She had been more than a sister. She had been his mother through the years of childhood. She hadn't stopped loving him, not ever. She hadn't stopped loving Father, even when she stormed at him for refusing to accept Communism. She had simply given up and gone away, because her visits to the old home were dangerous to her husband as well as her family. But Anna was lost, just the same. Lost, forever lost.

He heard the Professor cough. He raised his head.

"Is there anything further I can tell you?" he asked.

"Well, I'm still interested in your remarkable fluency in English. I didn't even know they taught it in Soviet schools."

"Oh, I didn't go to a state school, Professor. I went to a private school."

"A private school—in the Soviet Union?"

"That is right. You see, the Communists despised the middle-class people of Kiev—they called them 'bourgeois remnants of the czarist regime'—but they needed their help badly. So the middle-class people had some bargaining power. They demanded certain things, and one of them was the right to conduct a good private school for their children. That's where I first began to study English."

"When did you leave school, Pete?"

"When the Germans captured the city."

"Go on."

"Well, as I said, my father was sent to the Polish labor camp and I went with him. That's where I met Doctor Vlcek. He was a Czech university professor and a wonderful man—which is why the Germans sent him to a labor camp."

"They sent him there to teach?"

"Yes. The Germans can be very shrewd, you know. They don't want their laborers to rebel or escape, so they allow whole families to stay together, and they allow some education for the children. Doctor Vlcek taught regular classes, but he also found time to tutor students who were particularly good in some subjects—" Pyotr paused, feeling the heat of a blush on his face. "Or maybe he was just being kind when he gave special attention to me. I loved languages. I wanted to learn them all."

"What languages do you speak?"

"Russian, of course. English, fairly well. German, Czech, and Polish, passably. French, *un peu*—a little. But I would improve if I could just meet more French people."

"You will. You'll be shipped farther west into France."

Shipped, Pyotr thought, and his stomach shrank as if cold fingers had touched it. *Shipped* was the word the Germans used when they transferred slave labor from one camp to another. He said, "Does that mean I'll have to stay in a camp?"

"Well—"

"A camp with a high wire fence around it?"

"I don't know, Pete. It depends—"

"If they put me in a cage I'll break out," Pyotr said. "I'll never stay in a cage again. Never!"

The Professor and Bud Parente exchanged glances.

"He oughtn't to be cooped up, that's for sure," Bud said. "Maybe Battalion could use him as an interpreter."

"I'd be only too happy to serve," Pyotr said quickly. "I could question German prisoners. I could—"

The Professor shook his head.

"You're a foreign civilian, Pete, and you're too young. We wouldn't be allowed to use you."

Pyotr looked down at the floor. The little heat pills had almost burned themselves out.

"You'll like it in France," Bud said. "The frogs are pretty nice, for foreigners, and when the war's over they'll send you back to Russia."

"I don't want to go back to Russia," Pyotr said, suddenly rebellious.

"Why, Pete? It's your home, ain't it?"

"No—it's not my home any more."

The Professor sighed. "Well, as Bud says, you should like France, and maybe the French will let you stay there after the war."

Pyotr said nothing. What could he say?

He saw Bud yawn, and this set the Professor to yawning.

"Well," the Professor said, "I suppose we really should stop yakking and hit the sack."

"Yeah," Bud said, but in spite of his yawning he didn't sound enthusiastic.

Pyotr lay down in the hay. Bud snuffed the candle. Now the barn was dark again, but the darkness was alive with the heavy breathing, and here and there the snoring of American soldiers. Out on the ridge, German mortar shells were bursting at irregular intervals, harassing the American wire-cutting parties. In a few hours there would be another battle. More Americans would die—while he, a useless fifteen-year-old Russian boy, cowered in this barn, awaiting the outcome of the battle, awaiting his chance to spend more years in a cage. . . .

Well, maybe the French wouldn't put him in a cage, but they would keep him in one place, and find some kind of dull manual labor for him to do. He was a penniless foreign boy with no trade, so what else could he expect?

He had learned nothing new since he had last seen Doctor Vlcek. He had had no purpose, beyond mere escape, since his father had died. Now . . .

"Hey, kid."

"Yes?" Pyotr said.

"You been doing a lot of twisting and turning in that hay," Bud Parente said. "You having trouble getting to sleep?"

"Yes," Pyotr admitted. "I hope I haven't been bothering you."

"You haven't been bothering me," Bud said. "Hold on a minute."

Pyotr heard hay rustling. A moment later a candle flickered alight. Bud allowed the drippings to fall to the floor, and then he set the candle in the drippings. Pyotr watched him. Bud had a round face, chin blue with stubble, eyes brown and friendly. But he looked so tired.

"Can't sleep myself," Bud said in a low voice. "This business about a combat soldier being able to sleep whenever he wants to is a lot of boloney. When you been in the line long as I have it begins to get you."

"I can well imagine," Pyotr said. "It must be very hard on the nerves."

"It's worse than hard," Bud said. He rubbed his stomach. "I get butterflies in my belly before every attack."

Pyotr nodded. He felt sympathetic but he didn't know what to say.

"First it was the hedgerows," Bud said, as though speaking to himself. "Then Luxemburg. Then the Hürtgen Forest. Then the Bulge. Now Colmar." He laughed without making a sound. "I'm what they call a miracle man. That is, I'm still alive. I ain't even been hit yet. And in the Bloody Bucket that's pretty rare."

"The Bloody Bucket?" Pyotr said.

"The 28th Division," Bud said. "In case you don't already know it, that's the outfit you're with—Oboe Company, 112th Infantry, 28th Division."

"It's a fine outfit," Pyotr said.

"Best in the world." Bud sat hunched over, head lowered, staring at the candle. Then he raised his head and looked at Pyotr. "My old man's dead too," he said. "But when I was a kid he used to say, when you got troubles, the best way to forget 'em is to help somebody else out with *his* troubles."

Pyotr sat up straighter.

"Seems to me you got troubles," Bud said.

"Yes, but they're nothing compared to your—"

Bud made a slashing motion with his hand. "Like I said, I'm trying to forget my troubles. The thing is this, kid—do you want to stick with our outfit?"

The question took Pyotr completely by surprise. And yet the answer came out in the next breath.

"Yes!" he said.

"Uh-huh. I thought so." Bud rubbed his bristly blue chin. "The question is, how can we swing it? You got to earn your keep."

"I offered to be an interpreter," Pyotr said, "but—"

"That's for later, kid, after they learn to trust you. First you got to make yourself useful some other way." Bud scowled at the candle. "Permanent KP, maybe?"

"What is KP?"

"Kitchen Police. Helping the cooks around the company kitchen. I heard of some outfits that hired French civilian KPs, but the trouble is, when the outfits moved on they dropped the KPs. It's got to be something better than that, for a starter." Bud nibbled his thumbnail. "I'm going to talk to Captain Croft about you, and I want it to sound *good.*"

"What is Captain Croft like?" Pyotr asked.

"Smart. More educated than the Professor even. He's a rich man's son. But in spite of that he's a swell guy and the best company commander in the U. S. Army."

I have a chance, Pyotr thought. I have a chance. . . .

"But the gimmick," Bud said. "First we got to figure out a gimmick."

Pyotr didn't know exactly what a "gimmick" was, but he knew the game of chess. What he needed was a gambit, a way of gaining something by giving something. But what?

He thought back over the events of the day. What had he seen, looking from the barn window? Had he forgotten anything?

Suddenly he stiffened.

"Bud—would Sergeant Cotton like to know the location of a German headquarters?"

"Head—*what*?"

Bud's reaction was so violent that he knocked over the candle. Pyotr spoke into the darkness.

"I forgot to tell Sergeant Cotton a while ago. On the main street, just off the square, there is a large building that the Germans are using as a hospital. And across the street there is a smaller building which I think is some kind of headquarters—"

"Hold it!" Bud said. "Where's that candle?"

Bud made fumbling noises. Finally he lighted the candle. The Professor groaned and sat up, awakened by Bud's kick. Bud reached across him and punched Sergeant Cotton on the shoulder. Cotton's eyes opened, gray slits, fully alert.

"What is it?" he snapped.

"Bull, this kid spotted a kraut aid station this afternoon —and right across from it there's a CP!"

Bull Cotton sat up. He looked at Pyotr.

"All right, Russky. Talk."

Pyotr talked. After he finished, Bull Cotton stared at him for a long time.

"Kid," he said, "I haven't got a map of this town. There wasn't time before the attack to issue maps to all the platoons. And I can't wait till daylight for you to point out that CP from a barn window. If I don't get my platoon over to that raised road before dawn, the krauts are likely to occupy it to give themselves some flank security. Do you think you can see the CP from the road?"

"CP means headquarters?"

"Yeah. Command Post. Headquarters."

"I'm not sure," Pyotr said. "But I can surely see the aid station, as you call it. Will that be enough?"

"Yeah."

"Then I'll go to the road with you," Pyotr said.

The corners of Bull Cotton's mouth turned up in what might have been a smile.

"I better tell you," he said. "If the krauts also get the idea of occupying that road before daylight, they can mow us down while we're crossing the field."

Pyotr knew this without being told. He had known it all the while, and he was prepared.

"I'll take my chances," he said.

Bull Cotton looked at the Professor, then at Bud Parente. They nodded their heads.

"Some kid," Bull Cotton said, and lay back in the hay.

Bud winked at Pyotr.

"Now let's get some sleep," he said.

Chapter 5

A BOY TO LEAD THEM

At four o'clock in the morning—"0400," Bull Cotton called it—the platoon formed in the aisle of the barn.

"I want a column of squads," he said, "open squad column, first squad leading. If we run into fire we switch to a skirmish line, first squad on the right, fourth squad on the left. We take the road if we can. If we can't take it we fall back here and defend this barn. Everybody got that?"

There was a muffled chorus of mumbles.

"Okay, let's go."

Bull led the way outside, Pyotr, the Professor, and Bud close on his heels. Boots made a soft slush-slush in the snow as the squads followed in two long files. The barn fell behind, a vague white bulk in the darkness before dawn. Pyotr tapped Bull Cotton on his left arm. Bull swerved to the left. The swishing of boots was interrupted by a thump and a grunt as someone tripped and bumped into the man ahead of him. Pyotr tried to picture the field, the road, and the main street of town as he had seen them yesterday afternoon from the barn window, but he was not sure about anything now. He would just have to guess, and pray that the guess would be good enough. He counted off one hundred paces, then caught Bull Cotton by the arm.

"I think we're about to reach the little frozen brook," he whispered. "It runs through a pipe under the road and wanders across the field to about this point."

"Okay," Bull Cotton said. "Pass the word back."

Pyotr whispered to the Professor, who turned and whispered to Bud. The faint murmur ran down the line. A moment later Bull Cotton said, "This is it. Careful now."

Cautiously the column worked its way across the little gully. Saplings and bushes rustled against clothing but no one fell. "Now about four hundred paces straight ahead," Pyotr whispered to Bull.

Again, four hundred paces was just a guess—a rather wild one, at that—but Pyotr was doing the best he could. It seemed to take forever to count so many steps, but at last it was over. Bull Cotton stopped. Pyotr stopped beside him.

"Now turn right and keep going until you reach the road," Pyotr said.

Bull Cotton clamped his big hand around Pyotr's arm.

"Somebody has to stay here and make sure the men make the turn. That means you, Russky."

Pyotr understood. The column might come under fire as it approached the road, and Bull Cotton didn't want the death of a boy on his conscience.

He stood there, and as the men came to him he whispered, "Turn right." They kept coming, in two uneven files, until the last man reached him. He knew it was the last man when the fellow growled, "Tail guard," and then he was free to follow the column.

There was no sound in the night. None whatever. Even the German mortars had ceased to pound the ridge. Pyotr plodded on, counting steps. He didn't have to count steps now, because the road was directly ahead, and it didn't matter how many steps he took to reach it. But counting was something to do, something to occupy his mind. . . .

Three hundred and sixty-three, he thought, and bumped into the tail guard.

"We made it," the tail guard said. "Bull's over on the right flank. Just follow the embankment and you'll find him."

Following the embankment meant groping his way past thirty-odd men who seemed to have several hundred legs for him to trip over, but Pyotr kept going.

"Hi, boy," Bull Cotton said cheerfully. "Now all we have to do is stay put till dawn."

Dawn, Pyotr thought, and yielded to a temptation that had nagged him ever since he had been dragged out of a sound sleep at four o'clock in the morning.

"Sergeant," he said, "I understand that Oboe Company will attack at sunrise, and I understand why you have to get your men into position before the attack begins. But isn't three hours a rather long wait? I mean, after all the hurrying we've done—"

"Ha!" Bud Parente said wickedly in the darkness. "He's on to you already, Bull. Old Hurry-up-and-Wait Cotton, the pride of the U. S. Army!"

"At ease!" Bull Cotton whispered, but somehow it sounded like a bark. Also, as Pyotr had learned last night, "at ease" meant "shut up." He wished he hadn't asked that question, but when the sergeant spoke again his tone was quite reasonable.

"Listen, Russky, there are guys who spend thirty years in the Army without ever finding out why they have to hurry up and wait. But the reason is simple, see. I wanted to be here in time to clobber any krauts that might have ideas about occupying this road. And I wanted to make sure my own men didn't get clobbered. Now three hours is a long time to wait. Your feet will get awful cold. But you'll be alive at dawn—which you might not have been if we'd started out at five or six o'clock. Understand now, kiddo?"

"Yes," Pyotr said. "Thank you, sergeant."

"Think nothing of it," Bull Cotton said easily. Then he snarled, still in a whisper, "You, Parente! Go tell each squad

leader to post his BAR team in the ditch on the other side
of the road. On the double, foul-up!"

"Okay, okay," Bud said, and hurried away. Pyotr heard
him swear as he tripped over someone's legs, and then he
heard the Professor say, "Oh, that Bull. He's in fine form
this morning!"

After that, there was only silence and creeping cold.

Pyotr banged his shoes together, in imitation of everyone
else, but it didn't help. He was glad when Bud came back
in a talkative mood. This gave him a chance to ask about
weapons and combat. After Bud fell asleep, Pyotr waited,
just waited. He estimated that an hour went by. Then another hour. Bull Cotton ordered the whole platoon across
the road and into the ditch. Pyotr settled down next to
the Professor. He tried to wiggle his toes, but he could
not be sure they moved at all. I'm freezing, he thought.
He considered telling the Professor, but then, magically,
wrecked rooftops began to take shape before his doubting
eyes.

He looked upward. The sky had lightened. Dawn had
come.

A moment later, while he was still staring unbelievingly
at the jagged skyline, four shells screeched over the ridge
to the north. They burst hundreds of meters away, on the
edge of town; nevertheless, Pyotr buried his face in the
snow and held his hands over his ears.

A huge hand clamped on his shoulder.

"I said," Bull Cotton repeated, "is this the street we're
looking for?"

Pyotr squinted. At first he saw only a gray blur. Then
the street was there. He searched for familiar buildings,
but he recognized nothing.

"No," he shouted as more shells burst. "I must have made
a mistake."

"Crawl down the road with me," Bull Cotton roared in his ear. "We've got to find the right street."

Pyotr crawled after him, wondering forlornly if he should be crawling up the road, instead of down. Bull Cotton crawled fast, and in less than five minutes Pyotr was tired. But now, at least, he could feel. His hands and elbows and knees hurt, so he wasn't frozen after all. From time to time he glanced over the rim of earth beside the ditch. There was a street. He stopped. He racked his memory.

"Well?" Bull Cotton said.

"I think this is it," Pyotr said, "but I can't be sure. I can't see far enough—"

"We'll take a chance on it," Bull said. "Stay right here."

Pyotr stayed, while Bull crawled back to the platoon. Ten minutes later the platoon was strung out on either side of him, covering the mouth of the street.

"How about it, Russky?" Bull Cotton said.

"I still can't tell," Pyotr said. "If I could just see as far as the square—"

"Keeping looking," Bull ordered, and suddenly his voice was a shout in an otherwise soundless world. The shelling had stopped. But the world didn't remain soundless. Machine guns began to stutter. Some of them made a high-pitched, extremely rapid rattle; they were in the houses on the north side of town. Other guns sounded slower, deeper; they seemed to be on top of the ridge. Pyotr swiveled his head without raising it. He couldn't see the top of the ridge, but where the top of the ridge should be, little red eyes were winking. He let his gaze run downward until he came to the vineyards. Then he sensed, rather than saw, shadows, quick-darting shadows, among the vineyards, below the vineyards, shadows closing in on the town.

A ragged cheer arose from the platoon.

"Come on, Oboe Company!" Bud Parente yelled. "Come on, you beautiful bums!"

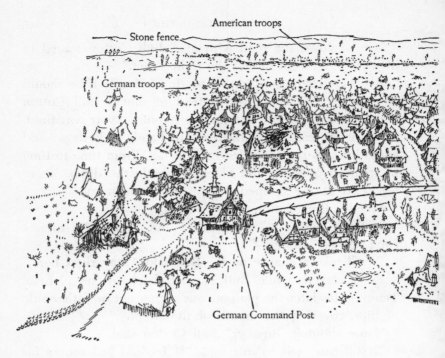

American troops

Stone fence

German troops

German Command Post

"Bud is a Dodger fan," the Professor said.

This remark made no sense whatever. Besides, Pyotr was too busy watching the zigzagging, disappearing, reappearing shadows. He could follow their movement to what looked like a stone wall near the bottom of the ridge, and then long, vicious red-yellow flashes began to lance out from the wall. He heard the *plop-plop-plop* of rifle fire, and the fast rattle of automatic weapons.

"BARs," the Professor said, and this time Pyotr understood. BARs were Browning Automatic Rifles. Each squad of American infantry had one BAR. Bull Cotton had four BARs right here in his platoon, but of course they hadn't opened fire yet.

Judging from the sound, Pyotr thought the men behind the stone wall must also have some machine guns. He asked the Professor about this.

"Yes, they have light machine guns too," the Professor

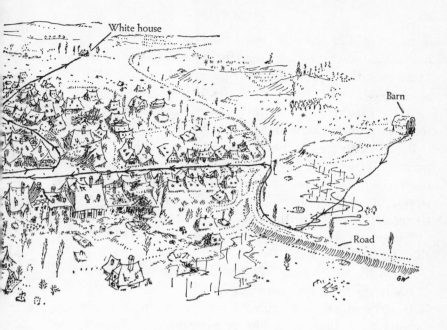

assured him. "The guns on top of the ridge are heavy, water-cooled weapons. They provide sustained covering fire. The light machine guns and BARs are ripping directly into those houses, and unless I miss my guess, something has to give pretty soon."

The five-shot bursts from the crest of the ridge, the deep-voiced American *rat-tat-tat* from the stone wall blended with the excited, metallic chattering of German MG-38s in the houses. But the American fire seemed to be building up, while the German fire slackened. As the Professor had said, something had to give.

"Why—" Pyotr began, and then raised his voice to a shout. "Why didn't the Germans defend the crest of the ridge in the first place? Wouldn't it have been easier to fire down at the Americans as they came uphill?"

"German psychology," the Professor shouted back. "They don't think the way we do. They often defend the reverse slope of a hill. Maybe they thought they could inflict heavier casualties by catching the attacking troops as they came over the skyline. But in this case they may have lost a town—"

"Hey, Russky!" It was Bull Cotton again. "Never mind the pretty fireworks. What do you see up this here street?"

Pyotr snapped his head around. He couldn't see the square. It was still too far away. He felt panicky. But maybe . . . He began to check the houses, examining the street, house by house. That big house on the left, he thought. It could be the one.

"Sergeant," he said, "I think I see it. The aid station, that is. If—"

"Wait till you're sure," Bull said in a deadly calm voice. "This is no time for guessing, boy."

Pyotr nodded miserably. Every man in the platoon seemed to be looking at him now, waiting impatiently for him to prove himself. He forgot the fire fight on the north side of town. He forgot everything but that street, emerging so slowly from the murk of dawn, the street with the mystery at the end, just beyond reach of his eyesight. Dimly he heard muttering. They probably were cursing him, and he couldn't blame them. But the only thing that mattered was the square. If there was a square at the end of this street, then the big house had to be the aid station, and if the big house was the aid station, then the CP had to be just across from it. If he could . . .

All at once, there it was. The square.

"I see it," he said.

Bull Cotton went on looking at him as if he hadn't spoken.

"I see it!" he shouted. "This is the right street!"

"Show me the house," Bull said.

Pyotr showed him. Bull nodded. Then he stood up. *"Third platoon,"* he said, *"let's go!"*

Pyotr looked around wildly. A hand touched his shoulder. "See you later, kid," Bud Parente said.

"I—" Pyotr didn't know what to say. He wanted to cry, "Take me with you!" but before he could utter the words the Professor said, "Keep your head down, Pete—and when you get a chance, make a beeline for that barn." And that seemed to settle it. The third platoon moved out. One moment they were all in the ditch with him, and then they were sliding down the embankment, entering the street. He reached out a hand to stop them, but they left him behind.

He lay in the ditch and watched them go. They moved fast, in two files, hugging the walls. Bull stopped them once, three houses short of the aid station. Then they went forward again.

Suddenly a machine pistol snarled. Bull vanished into a doorway. The short man immediately behind him also tried to reach the doorway, but the machine pistol stuttered out another burst and the little man dropped his carbine, clutched at his chest, and slumped to the ground.

"*Bud,*" Pyotr said aloud: "*They killed Bud!*"

But now a BAR and a dozen rifles were firing at the house which concealed the burp gunner. A faint shout reached Pyotr's ears: "Grenade!" The Americans near the house threw themselves to the ground, and then the window to the right of the doorway spouted smoke and flame. The shout of "Grenade!" sounded again, and this time the window left of the doorway erupted. Pyotr could hear Bull's voice giving orders, but he couldn't make out the words. The men on the ground all got up and began running forward, firing their weapons from the hip. In a matter of seconds they reached the aid station. The big BAR man in the lead fired a burst at the door, and then the Americans crowded inside.

Pyotr couldn't see the CP, but he knew that the men across the street must have rushed that house also. Now there were only a few Americans out in the open, and they seemed to be acting as guards. The aid station and the CP had been taken. Pyotr pulled off his wool hat, and wiped his forehead with his coat sleeve. He was sweating.

He looked toward the north end of town. Now he could see the stone wall distinctly. The muzzle flashes were less bright—in fact, they were almost invisible—but some Americans had advanced from the wall and begun firing from small outbuildings closer to the houses where the Germans had set up their first line of defense. Once the Americans reached the houses, this attack would be a hand-to-hand affair, a grim battle from house to house until all of the Germans were either dead or prisoners.

But he would have no part in it.

Behind him, the snowy field was empty. He could go back to the barn now. He could climb the stepladder again and watch the whole action until it ended.

No, he thought. They killed Bud. I've got to *do* something.

Do what?

Restlessly, he turned his head to the left. The night before last, suffering under the burden of a heavy ration box, he had supposed that the road went for several hundred meters through the heart of town. Yesterday morning, viewing the road from the barn window, he had realized that it served as a street for only a comparatively short distance. At both ends of town, the road curved outward like the horns of a bull. . . .

He stiffened.

Two long files of men were marching up the road from the south!

Without pausing for a second thought, Pyotr dived over the rim of the ditch and rolled down the embankment. He picked himself up and started running. His shoes clattered on the cobblestones. He passed the small huddled form of

Bud Parente. As he came to the doorway of the house next to the aid station, an arm snaked out and coiled around his waist. The arm lifted him off the ground but he kept on trying to run, feet churning the air.

"Hey!" the guard shouted. "What's wrong with you?"

"Bull!" Pyotr gasped. "Where's Bull?"

"In the CP. What—"

"Germans!" Pyotr yelled. "Hundreds of Germans, coming this way!"

The guard set him down. He dashed across the street. He rushed through the open doorway of the CP and skidded to a stop. Bull Cotton, the Professor, and two squad leaders were sitting in chairs on one side of a big table. Behind them stood several riflemen, weapons in hand. Across the table, an *Oberleutnant*—equal in rank to an American first lieutenant—a feldwebel, and half a dozen ordinary soldiers of a German field division slumped in attitudes of beaten weariness. The bodies of two German officers lay sprawled near a blown-in window. A telephone switchboard lay smashed on the floor. Two field radios also had been wrecked. Pyotr panted, catching his breath. Bull Cotton scowled at him.

"What are you doing here, Russky?"

"Germans," Pyotr said. "Hundreds of Germans, coming up the road from the south!"

Bull Cotton looked at him with those cold gray eyes.

"How many Germans, Russky?"

"Well—a hundred, at least."

"One short-handed company," Bull Cotton said. He stood up. "Norton, Schmidt, collect the platoon and fall them in on the street. Professor, you're in charge of these." He jerked his thumb at the prisoners. "Herd them along behind the platoon, and if any of them even looks like making a break, let him have it."

Outside, half of the platoon had already fallen in. More

men poured out of the aid station, the basement of the CP, and other nearby buildings. Pyotr glanced at the Professor, who seemed to be fretting about his prisoners, but stayed with Bull Cotton. Bull raised his arm high, then whipped it forward as if he were throwing a stone. "Double time," he barked, and the platoon followed him at a trot.

Just short of the end of the street, Bull Cotton raised his arm again. The platoon clattered to a halt. Pyotr was astonished when the sergeant caught him by the arm and pulled him along to the edge of the last house.

"Now show me," Bull Cotton said.

Pyotr poked his head around the edge of the house. "There," he said.

The Germans were not more than five hundred meters away. They were moving fast.

"The question is," Bull said, "are they just going to reinforce the krauts at the north end of town, or are they going to follow the road and outflank Oboe Company?"

Pyotr glanced over his shoulder. The road swung away from town, past the stone wall where he had last seen Oboe Company in action.

"If I were the German commander," he said, "I'd stay on the road and attack Oboe Company from the side. Except that I wouldn't stay on the road all the way. I would leave it soon and use the embankment as a shield."

Bull Cotton chuckled.

"We call it cover and concealment," he said. "And if the kraut CO knows his business, that's exactly what he'll do."

Pyotr looked upward. Bull's face was directly above his own, calmly watching the Germans advance. But he couldn't just stand there and watch them. . . .

"I'll give them another hundred yards," Bull Cotton said. "If they follow the road into town, they're going to reinforce. If they leave the road before they hit town, they're going to try a flank attack."

Pyotr felt faint. He yawned, sucked in a breath, and realized that he hadn't been breathing at all. He breathed deeply and felt better. He closed his strained eyes and opened them again. The Germans were leaving the road!

"Thought so," Bull Cotton said, and dragged Pyotr back to the platoon. The four squad leaders were assembled in a little group. They said nothing. They just looked at Bull Cotton.

"We're going to sneak along the edge of town, this side of the road embankment," Bull said. "Reason is, a company of krauts is doing the same thing on the other side of the road. We can't be sure they won't spot us, though, so I want all the men to carry their rifles at the carry—"

"Carry?" Sergeant Norton said. "What for, Bull?"

"Because we always carry our rifles at high port, and the krauts always carry theirs at the carry. And if we do get spotted, I want them to think we're Germans instead of Americans. Now you got that straight?"

"Yeah," Norton said.

"Okay, then get *this* straight. This kid is going to lead us to the best position to stop those krauts. He spent a whole day in that barn out there watching this town. And he *knows* it."

Everybody looked at Pyotr.

"But—but I don't remember," he stammered. "I—"

"You better remember," Bull Cotton said. "You're the only one here that knows anything about this town."

Pyotr stood there in a state of shock. Bull Cotton took him by the shoulders, turned him until he was facing north, and gave him a shove. He began walking. He glanced to the rear. Bull Cotton was practically breathing down his neck. And behind Bull, the third platoon was following in single file.

I must remember, he thought. If I don't remember I'll lead them into a death trap.

For a while there was only the numbness that came from having a terrible responsibility thrust upon him. But as he walked forward, something stirred in his memory.

The little white house, he thought.

He could see it now, in his mind's eye. It was quite close to the road embankment, and so far removed from the rows of houses where the Germans had set up their line of defense that they probably hadn't occupied it. To reach the little house, he had to pass the German-occupied houses, and then pass the end of the stone wall where the Americans were lodged. But he couldn't do it safely by following the road embankment. The space between the road and the town was too open. He must guide the platoon farther into town, and then, just before he reached the area where the fighting was going on, he must swing back toward the road. Once he reached that point, there was a dangerous space of a hundred meters or more to cross, all in the open.

But he would cross it when he came to it.

One way or the other, he must reach the little white house. This much he knew.

He told Bull about the house. Bull's eyes glinted.

"Okay, Russky. Lead the way."

"Here we turn left," Pyotr said. The strength of his own voice surprised him. He stepped boldly into the narrow, winding street that would end in battle.

Chapter 6

RUN TO THE LITTLE WHITE HOUSE

As far as the first turn, it was just a matter of putting one foot in front of the other and going forward. But once he rounded the turn, Pyotr saw a jumbled pile of stones and beams rearing up like a small mountain. Two whole houses had collapsed, blocking the street.

"I didn't realize—" he began shakily.

"Neither did I," Bull Cotton said. "But we can't go back now. Start climbing, Russky."

Pyotr put his foot on a big stone, caught hold of a projecting beam, and hauled himself upward. Almost immediately the shakiness left his legs. He could climb. If he kept his mind on climbing alone, he would be all right. . . . His foot slipped. He slid backward, clutching at thin air. A huge hand clamped on his arm, stopping him. Bull Cotton growled, "Take it easy, boy. You almost kicked me in the teeth." Pyotr gasped out an apology and continued to climb. In another minute he was on top of the mound of rubble. He turned around and looked downward.

Some of the heavier men were having trouble, but they were all coming up as fast as they could. Except for the Professor. The Professor was still standing on the cobblestones below, anxiously watching the progress of his prisoners. He must be afraid they would escape.

"Sergeant Cotton," Pyotr said, and pointed.

Bull Cotton made a grunting noise that could have been a laugh, and said, "Come on up, Prof. I've got them covered."

The Professor slung his carbine on his shoulder and scrambled up the pile of ruins so energetically that he passed his own prisoners. "Now let's get down off this thing," Bull said.

Going down the far side was easy. Bull nodded at Pyotr and Pyotr went on ahead. The narrow street took another turn to the left, and a new worry seized him.

"We're going too far into the center of town," he said. "I didn't realize—"

"Don't say that again!" Bull Cotton barked. "Just keep on going!"

There was nothing else to do.

The street meandered even farther toward the center of town. German machine guns snarled, louder and louder. Then another mountain of rubble had to be scaled. Pyotr was sweating, panting, as he slid down the far side. He stopped and brushed a hand across his eyes. Ah! Now the street was veering to the right. He went ahead again.

The street continued to swing to the right, toward the road embankment, away from the houses full of Germans. The next pile of stones and timber was smaller, easier to climb. Pyotr eased himself down to the cobblestones. Up ahead, the houses had wide spaces between them, and there weren't many houses left.

He looked at Bull Cotton. Bull nodded. Then he raised his arm and made rapid circling motions. The platoon gathered around him.

"From here on out," he said, "we leave the street and sneak through back yards. We rush from house to house, by squads. When we get to the last house in the row, we assemble. That's enough for now. First squad—take off!"

The first squad circled to the rear of the nearest house.

"Bull," the Professor said, "what about these prisoners?"

"Go ahead of the third squad," Cotton said. "You too, Russky. I'll bring up the fourth squad myself."

The first squad made a running dash to the next house. The second followed. Pyotr stayed close to the Professor, and he ran with the prisoners when their turn came. The German privates were white-faced and fearful, which was only natural for men who could neither fight nor protect themselves. The feldwebel swore monotonously as he ran. The tall oberleutnant swung along easily, suffering his humiliation in dignified silence. Pyotr watched the officer carefully, but he knew that the third and fourth squads, coming along close behind, could easily shoot down any prisoner who tried to escape.

Up the line, house by house, the platoon made its way. Not a shot was fired until the first squad rushed the last house. Pyotr heard a distant chattering, and bullets ricocheted from the stone wall up ahead, whining viciously as they careened away in the cold air. The first squad reached the rear of the house and stopped. The second squad made its rush, and again the German weapon chattered. This time one of the ricochets howled like a dying cat. Pyotr shuddered, partly from fear and partly because the sound put his teeth on edge.

"Let's take a break," the Professor said.

Pyotr studied the Professor. He had already marked the schoolteacher as a worrier, a nervous individual, but now the anxiety did not show. There stood the Professor, holding his little group of prisoners together, talking so calmly —and smiling!

"That's just a burp gun," the Professor said. "It's beyond range to hit anybody, except by accident. We've got a saying about the burp gun. We say, if the first slug misses you, they all do." He turned casually to the oberleutnant. "How about that, lieutenant?"

The oberleutnant frowned at the Professor. Then, unexpectedly, he eked out a thin smile.

"Unfortunately," he said in heavily accented but good

English, "it is true. Our Schmeisser pistol has neither the range nor the accuracy of your excellent automatic rifle."

"There," the Professor said, winking at Pyotr. "You see? Now all we have to do—"

"Hey, Professor!" Bull Cotton shouted. "Get those kraut-heads moving!"

The Professor sighed. "As I was saying, all we have to do is run to the next house, more or less safely. Now let's go."

He gestured with his carbine, and the six German privates streaked for the next house. The feldwebel, the ober-leutnant, the Professor, and Pyotr followed in a group. The burp gun chattered. Pyotr saw snow spurt, barely six paces in front of him. The mad chattering resumed. The burp gun might not be accurate, but it fired so fast!

The feldwebel took another running step, flung out his arms, and dived into the snow.

Pyotr ran on, heart pounding. Then he stopped. He did not know why. He wheeled around and looked back.

The Professor and the oberleutnant were stooping over the fallen man. Pyotr saw the Professor sling his carbine and bend down to grasp the feldwebel under the arms, but the oberleutnant pushed him away. With one quick surge of strength, the tall German officer lifted the wounded non-com and draped him over his shoulder like a sack of wheat. Then he began running toward the house. Pyotr whirled and sprinted on.

He heard the burp gun rip off another burst. Bullets spattered against stone and sang off into space. Pyotr gained the rear wall of the house and collided with a big German private. The man held him, scarcely noticing him, looking over his head. Pyotr freed himself and turned around. The oberleutnant was running heavily with his burden, and the Professor was keeping pace with him, shar-ing the danger. The burp gun rattled again, and again. More bullets screeched off the wall. Then suddenly the oberleutnant and the Professor were behind the wall, safe.

The oberleutnant lowered the feldwebel to the ground and kneeled beside him.

"Through the chest," he said, indicating a tear in the feldwebel's coat. "High in the chest, however. He may live."

"Good," the Professor gasped. He bent over the feldwebel, who was gritting his teeth against the pain. "He must be a good man, lieutenant, for you to do that."

"He is a good man," the oberleutnant said gently. Then he jabbed his finger at two privates. "You, Schwenke! And you, Kraus! Stand by to carry him!"

Each word cracked like a pistol shot. The two privates came over to the feldwebel and stood waiting. The Professor smiled wryly.

"Courage is courage wherever you find it," he said to Pyotr, "but I'm sure glad he isn't an officer in our army."

Pyotr nodded absently. He was watching the third squad make its run across the open space. The burp gun continued its angry snarling, but nobody was hit. The fourth squad came in carrying a man who had been shot through the upper leg. The platoon gathered around Bull Cotton. Bull squinted at the little white house that stood a hundred and fifty meters away, and nodded grimly.

"They're bound to spot us," he said, "even if that burp gunner hasn't already tipped them off. So what I want is this. First squad, go upstairs in this here house and cover for the rest of the platoon. The minute the platoon reaches the white house, it covers for the first squad. When we all get there I want the second and third squads in the house itself, and the first and fourth squads ranged along the garden wall, facing the embankment. Reason is, I don't want the whole platoon cooped up in one house when the fire fight starts." Bull paused. "Any questions?"

Nobody spoke.

"First squad, upstairs," Bull said.

The first squad disappeared into the house. Pyotr heard boots pounding on stairsteps. He heard glass crash and tinkle as weapons smashed through windows. Then there was silence.

"We move out in squad diamonds," Bull said. "We carry our weapons at high port now because I don't want us to draw any American fire. Anybody gets hit, we pick him up and carry him, no matter what. You all set?"

Pyotr looked at the strained faces around him. He drew in a long breath and held it. He saw Bull Cotton raise his arm and whip it forward. The second squad began its rush. The third squad followed immediately. And then suddenly he was running, crouched over, seeing only the snow directly in front of his feet, yet sensing the little white house up ahead, so close, yet so very far away.

For the first few seconds he heard nothing but the thud of boots, the labored breathing of running men. Then came the high-pitched rattle of a German machine gun. It was just one among many German guns, yet he knew instinctively that it was closer than the others, and that it was firing at him. The muscles of his back clenched into hard ridges. His breath came in gasps that hurt his lungs. But nothing happened. He threw a glance over his shoulder. For a moment all he saw was the fourth squad, coming along a few paces behind him. And then two men lurched and fell in the snow.

"Hit the dirt!" someone yelled.

Pyotr plunged headlong. He heard more yelling behind him. At first he didn't dare move. But the yelling went on, so he raised his head and looked to the rear. The whole fourth squad was hugging the ground. One man was clutching the small of his back, rocking from side to side, groaning in agony. Only two heads were up—those of Bull

Cotton and the squad leader. They were trying to locate that German gun.

"I can't spot it," the squad leader yelled.

"Neither can I," Bull shouted in return. He began to pound the ground with his fist. "What's wrong with that first squad? Are they blind? We'll be pinned down all day if—"

A hearty, stuttering roar came from an upstairs window in the house the first squad had occupied. The BAR growled again. The German machine gun stopped firing.

"A-h-h-h!" Pyotr said, and the same sighing groan of relief rose all around him.

"Professor," Bull Cotton said, "get two of your krauts to basket-carry Thompson."

The Professor jumped to his feet.

"Get up!" he said. "Get up, all of you!"

The prisoners cowered in the snow.

"Get up!" the Professor shouted. He bent down, seized a gray collar, and began to shake the man.

"Never mind that," the oberleutnant said. And then, in German, he raged at his men. He called them cowardly swine. He kicked them. They scrambled to their feet in panic.

"Now what is a basket-carry?" he asked Bull Cotton.

Bull leaped over to the Professor. His big left hand grasped the Professor's right wrist. His right hand wrapped around the Professor's left wrist. The Professor's slim hands closed about Bull's wrists. Together they stood supporting an invisible wounded man.

"Two hands locked low, under his legs," Bull said. "Two hands locked high, behind his back. This way you can carry him in a sitting position."

"So?" The oberleutnant shrugged. "We do it the same way." He pointed to the American who had been shot in the back. "You, Danner. And you, Kresge. Pick him up!"

The two German privates rushed to obey. Thompson, the wounded American, screamed once as they lifted him, then slumped unconscious in their arms. Bull stepped over to a soldier who lay motionless in the snow. The soldier's helmet had fallen off and Pyotr could see that he was blond and very young. Bull opened the boy's coat, then his shirt. He nodded slowly. He thrust his hand deeper inside the brown shirt and pulled out two metal discs. He yanked one disc off the chain that encircled the boy's neck and straightened up. "If I sprain an ankle or something," he said, "you'll find one of Jimmy's dog tags in my pocket."

The squad leader picked up Jimmy's rifle. He drew the bayonet from its scabbard and fixed it to the muzzle of the rifle. He jabbed the bayonet into the ground and placed Jimmy's helmet on the rifle butt. When he turned around his face showed no expression whatever.

"We better go, Bull," he said.

Bull whipped his hand forward.

The platoon moved toward the white house, not running now, just trotting with rifles held high in the American fashion. German machine guns rattled on, but the volume of fire from the Americans behind the stone fence had slackened.

They're watching us, Pyotr thought. I hope they can see that we're Americans.

A chorus of whooping yells came from the stone fence. The Americans had recognized their own!

And there was the little white house.

Chapter 7

Small though it seemed, the house was two stories high. Built of whitewashed stone, it looked like a fort. Two men flung their combined weight against the closed door. They bounced back, grunting.

"Shoot the lock off," Bull Cotton said.

A BAR and several rifles blasted at the lock. The heavy door creaked inward as if opened by an unseen hand. The second and third squads crowded inside, stumbling, bumping into each other, awkward in their anxiety to get upstairs and take firing positions at the windows. The fourth squad peeled off to the left, seeking cover behind the garden wall. Pyotr flattened his nose against a broad gray back as the prisoners jammed up in the doorway. Then he was inside, following the prisoners and the wounded through the parlor, into the kitchen, and down a short, steep flight of stairs.

The cellar was a dark, dank little room with dingy stone walls and a bare earthen floor. Against the far wall, one bin contained several sacks of potatoes, and another a few scattered lumps of low-grade coal. The only item of furniture was a crude table, littered with garden tools and a sorry collection of canned goods. Pyotr stopped on the stairs. There were too many men down here. They seemed to fill the space, leaving no air. He felt trapped.

The Professor stepped over to the table and swept the tools and cans to the floor.

"Lay the wounded here," he said. Then his thin face

twisted in a grimace of doubt. "No, wait. We ought to get
some clean sheets to lay them on."

Pyotr whirled around and bounded upstairs. He dashed
through the kitchen and into the short hallway that led to
the parlor. Here it was—the big linen chest. He flung open
the chest, saw piles of white cloth, and scooped up an arm-
ful. He turned and almost bumped into the Professor.

"Tablecloths," the Professor said. "Oh, well, they'll do."

He took the tablecloths from Pyotr and ran downstairs.
Pyotr started to follow, but the hoarse stutter of a BAR
brought him to a halt. Had the attack begun already? No.
The BAR was firing from a back window, covering the advance of the first squad to this house. He rushed to the door
and looked out. There they came, running hard—and carrying two wounded men!

Pyotr raced through the house and halfway down the
cellar stairs.

"Professor!" he shouted. "They're bringing in two more
wounded men! We'll need mattresses down here!"

The Professor stared at him. "Yes, of course," he murmured. "Mattresses. But—" He made a vague gesture with
his carbine toward the German prisoners.

"There is no way for us to escape now," the oberleutnant
said in a dry voice. "Let us go upstairs and obtain mattresses before the attack begins."

"All right," the Professor said. "You and three of your
men—"

Pyotr didn't wait to hear more. He ran up to the second
floor and burst into the first room he came to. Bull Cotton,
two riflemen, and a BAR man were kneeling at the front
windows. Bull swiveled his head around.

"What are you doing here, boy?"

"We need mattresses," Pyotr said. "They're bringing in
more wounded."

"How many?"

"Two."

Bull's big body drooped. Then he straightened.

"There's the beds," he said.

Two high four-poster beds filled half of the room. They were fully made, their blue-and-white spreads drawn smooth and taut by the tidy French housewife who had had to abandon this comfortable home. Poor woman, Pyotr thought. He threw a spread and a bolster to the floor. He dug his hands deep into the mattress and pulled hard.

Suddenly he was flat on his back, buried under a billowing, weightless white mass. He spluttered, thrashing wildly. The oberleutnant's face appeared above him.

"That will teach you not to provoke a feather mattress," the oberleutnant said. "Go downstairs, boy."

Pyotr picked himself up. The oberleutnant and one of his men passed him, carrying the enormous, feather-stuffed mass with the greatest of ease. The two other Germans stripped the second bed and went through the door.

Pyotr stood alone, feeling foolish.

"Get out of here," Bull Cotton said.

Pyotr went downstairs, but slowly. In the little hallway he met four members of the first squad, carrying their wounded. One of the wounded men moaned. Pyotr stopped. He didn't want to go down into that cellar. He stood in the hallway, wondering where he could go. The four men from the first squad passed him again. They had to go outside and fight. But what did he have to do?

Nothing. Except go down into that crowded, airless cellar and watch men in pain.

He plodded down the cellar steps. The mattresses had been placed on the floor and a wounded soldier lay on each mattress. The Germans were stripping them, making ready to tend their wounds. Pyotr glanced at the table. The Professor and the oberleutnant were bending over the soldier

named Thompson. They had stripped him to the waist, and
now they were pulling down his trousers.

The trousers were soaked with blood. Thompson's woolen
underwear was drenched, soggy red. When the underwear
came off Pyotr saw the hole in Thompson's abdomen.
Every time Thompson breathed, blood came welling out of
that raw, round hole.

Pyotr lowered his head.

"It went all the way through," the Professor was saying,
"from back to front. We'll have to apply two bandages—
and just hope he lasts."

The Professor tore open his own first-aid kit. The oberleutnant picked up Thompson's cartridge belt and opened
its kit. Now each had a large white bandage in his hands.
Black spots appeared on the bandages. The spots began to
dance. Pyotr closed his eyes. The spots weren't on the bandages, they were in his eyes.

"He won't last long," the oberleutnant said, "with a
punctured kidney and intestines."

Pyotr felt himself falling. He threw out both arms. One
hand whacked against a stairstep just before his face struck
it. Pain shot blindingly upward, from his cheekbone, from
his nose, into a cavern between his temples. The pain
pounded and boiled like an ocean wave, stretching his
skull. Just when his head seemed about to burst the wave
retreated, drained downward, settled in his cheek and nose.
He lifted his head, opened his eyes, and saw blood dripping on the rough board of the stairstep. His stomach
heaved. He swallowed and began climbing. He stumbled
through the hallway, dripping blood, until he came to the
kitchen. At the sink he soaked a towel with cold water and
held it against his nose with one hand while he fingered his
cheekbone with the other. It wasn't broken. But what a
sorry specimen he was, for a doctor's son. He couldn't stand
the sight of blood. Every time . . .

"Get set!" Bull Cotton's shout filled the entire house. "They're ready to roll!"

Pyotr dropped the towel. He bounded through the hallway into the parlor. There were two narrow front windows with blinds half drawn. He dropped to his knees, crawled to the right-hand window, and peered out.

There they were!

Half a dozen blurry black blobs on the railroad embankment took firm shape—coal-scuttle helmets, some motionless, some moving. They were observing, scanning this house, the garden wall, the well, the shed, every rock and stump and ditch and hole between them and the main American position behind that fence back there. They had flanked Oboe Company and now they were ready to attack.

"Hold your fire until they're over the embankment," Bull Cotton said, and though he now spoke in a normal voice, every word carried to every room. Pyotr wondered how the men out in the yard could know. Then he remembered. Hand signals from the side windows, of course. One of the coal-scuttle helmets disappeared. That meant the German was reporting to his commander. A minute more, just a minute more.

Pyotr ran his tongue between his gums and his swollen upper lip. As the tongue passed beneath his nose he thought: It's stopped bleeding; there's a crust on my upper lip that crinkles when I move it.

And then the Germans came.

They swept over the top of the embankment and down the steep snowy slope, digging in their heels to keep from sliding. Some of them slid anyway, and one man lost his footing and tumbled to the bottom. It all seemed very natural and human, but even in his excitement Pyotr could see the workmanlike formations of squads, the wide intervals between men, the fast and deadly certainty of a veteran infantry company advancing to the attack. What's more, they were not advancing in lines, but in a wide, loose column, heading straight for the house.

After a spasm of fear, Pyotr wondered why. Ever since he had thought of this house as a fort for the third platoon, he had worried about the possibility that the Germans would bypass it entirely, leaving Bull Cotton's men with nothing but distant targets to shoot at. That possibility hadn't bothered Bull, however, and obviously the German commander also valued the house. Why? What was so significant about this small, isolated white building that Pyotr had picked out in hopeful ignorance?

In an abrupt closing movement, the German column narrowed its front. Now it was no wider than the house itself— and Pyotr understood. Empty, this house would provide an ideal screen between the Germans and the American position behind the stone fence. Empty, it would shield the Germans from direct fire until they were halfway to their objective.

But it was *not* empty, and if it held . . .

If it held!

Pyotr could see the faces beneath those coal-scuttle helmets. They seemed so white. One thin fellow out in front had an oddly fat face. Every time he took a step, his jowls shook.

He was so *close*.

He'll see me, Pyotr thought, and ducked.

"Let 'em have it!" Bull Cotton said.

Upstairs, windowpanes burst outward with one great shattering crash. Pyotr raised his head in time to see two chairs land in the snowy yard. He stared at them, dumfounded. He hadn't even thought about windowpanes until this instant. Why had Bull waited . . . ? Before the question took full form, the jackhammer chorus of four BARs and twenty-odd M-1 rifles blasted it from Pyotr's mind. In a weird, dreamlike, timeless span of time, he saw a whole company of German infantry frozen in place, like living statues. Somehow the many white, upraised faces out there fused into one face. He was watching a young German soldier directly in front of him. The boy stood spread-legged, jaw hanging, mouth open, round horrified eyes fixed on an upstairs window, rifle trailing uselessly from one hand. Then the boy's jaw firmed, and his mouth closed, and he seemed to have made a decision. He placed the butt of the rifle on the ground. He sank to his knees, still grasping the rifle. He leaned forward and slowly, gently, lowered himself into the snow.

He looked so tired, deciding to die.

German soldiers were falling to the ground everywhere. They crumpled singly, in pairs, by threes. They fell so fast that Pyotr's eyes could not register their fall. And the rest just stood there, unable to move. Oh, help them, he thought, but guiltily he realized that this was not what he should be thinking. He closed his eyes, opened them again. Now a soldier was raising his arm, throwing something. Pyotr watched it come toward the house, end over end. There seemed to be a stick, a handle, and there was a hazy blob attached to the handle. The thing looked like a potato masher.

A potato masher!

Pyotr sprawled on the floor just as the potato-masher grenade exploded against the wall of the house. The concussion picked him up and thumped him down again. He thought, I am deaf, but then the giant popcorn roaster of rapid fire told him that he wasn't. He raised his upper body. Shards of glass showered to the floor. The grenade had blown in both front windows and the side window too. He rose to his knees, shaking off splinters of glass, and blood from his nose trickled down into his open mouth.

He spat, wiped his nose with his sleeve, and went back to the window.

Germans were running toward the embankment, throwing away rifles and automatic pistols, scrambling madly upward, using both hands and feet. The BARs and M-1s kept up their murderous din. Fleeing Germans slipped or toppled down the snowy slope. Some got up again, climbed the embankment, and disappeared. Some lay broken and twisted at the bottom of the slope. A few made small, helpless movements. It was the difference between those who had merely slipped and fallen, those who were dead, and those who wished they were.

There must be fifty of them out there, Pyotr thought. No, more than fifty. Many more.

It came to him then: the reason Bull Cotton had waited until the last moment to smash the windowpanes. He had wanted the thin wintry sun to shine on unbroken glass. He had wanted the house to seem innocent until the Germans walked into his trap. This grisly massacre was the result.

The rifles and BARs out in the yard fell silent. Upstairs, two or three rifles kept on popping, and one BAR spat vengefully through a side window.

"What's wrong with you guys?" Bull Cotton yelled. "Cease firing!"

The BAR ripped off a five-shot burst, then stopped.

Silence settled over the scene like a chill blanket. At the foot of the embankment, a single voice cried, *"Mutter! Mutter!"* again and again.

Mutter meant Mother. Pyotr covered his ears, but he could still hear the weak, wailing voice. He lowered his hands from his ears and stood up. He wobbled.

"Bull," someone upstairs said, "there's some of them hiding behind the well. That's what we were shooting at."

"*They* ain't shooting," Bull said. "Give 'em a chance to give up, will you?"

Pyotr looked at the well. The well itself was all he saw. He cleared his throat.

"Sergeant Cotton!"

"Yeah, Russky. You all right, boy?"

"I am quite well, thank you. And I speak German, sergeant."

"Oh. Well, tell them to come out reaching, Russky."

"Reaching?"

"With their hands up, kid."

"Yes, sergeant. But—will you please—"

"Nobody's going to shoot them, Russky. You just call out now, loud and strong."

Pyotr filled his chest with air.

"German soldiers!" he shouted. "Come out and surrender! Come out with your hands raised!"

Three German helmets rose above the rim of the well. Then, unexpectedly, two poked around the side of the shed, and four appeared over the edge of the ditch. One of the men in the ditch shouted "*Kamerad! Kamerad!*" and the man next to him told him to shut up. Instead of raising their hands, they locked fingers behind their helmets, but they all came out into the open.

The wounded man at the foot of the embankment went on calling for his mother.

"Sergeant Cotton—" Pyotr said, but before he could say more Bull Cotton came bounding downstairs. Bull threw open the door and went outside. Pyotr trotted after him.

Bull strode toward the garden wall. The men of the first squad were all lined up behind the wall, but there didn't seem to be many of them. Only seven. And now Schmidt, the short, keg-bodied squad leader came forward, frowning.

"What's up, Tubby?" Bull asked quietly.

"Listen," Schmidt said in a gravel-voiced whisper, "I only got five men—"

"Six, Tubby. Can't you count?"

"I sure can. I lost two yesterday. And two more running over here. And Grinstead caught it just as the last of them krauts was going over the embankment. He got up too quick and one of them must of turned around long enough to pot him through the head. And then there's Polski. He don't act right, Bull. I think he's had it."

Pyotr looked over his shoulder. Five men were leaning idly against the wall, watching the sergeants. The sixth, a bear-sized, bear-shaped fellow, stood staring into space. The fourth squad had fanned out from the other side of the house to collect the advancing prisoners, but the big brown bear who must be Polski ignored them.

"Yeah," Bull said, "he looks bad, Tubby."

"First he couldn't locate that burp gunner that had you pinned down on the way here. I had to point the guy out to him. And then when the krauts came over the embankment it was the same thing all over again. It was like he couldn't *see* them. I had to boot him—"

"Okay, Tubby. Give his BAR to someone else. Think he can guard prisoners?"

Schmidt glanced at the Germans. They were standing meekly while the fourth squad searched them.

"From the looks of them a kid could do it," Schmidt said. "I bet *this* kid could, anyway."

Pyotr smiled gratefully at Tubby Schmidt. And then the German soldier called for his mother.

"What's wrong, Russky?"

"Sergeant, that boy out there. Can't you *do* something—"

"Easy, Pete. Easy, boy."

Bull Cotton put his heavy hand on Pyotr's shoulder, and Pyotr stopped squirming. This was the first time Bull had called him Pete since they had met in the barn. And he

knew why. Russky was the nickname he must expect and
accept, most of the time. But when he needed a strong
hand and a warm voice to steady him, Bull would call him
Pete.

He smiled up at his big friend, Wayne Cotton.

Whereupon, Sergeant Bull Cotton slapped him on the
back and bawled: "Norton! On the double!"

Sergeant Norton, leader of the fourth squad, came running. By the time he arrived, Pyotr had recovered from
Bull's backslap.

"I want all the kraut wounded brought to the house,"
Bull told Norton and Schmidt.

"But Bull," Norton objected, "suppose they come over the
embankment again. Or suppose they lay back and clobber
us with mortars. If they catch us in the open—"

"Forget it," Bull said. "They're through here. The only
thing they can do now is go back and reinforce the krauts
in the town. And the only thing we can do is join up
with our own guys behind that fence out there."

Norton looked at Schmidt.

"He's right," Schmidt said.

"Call Polski over here," Bull said.

Schmidt turned his head. "Polski!"

Polski didn't move.

"Hey, Polski! Come—"

"Never mind," Bull said. "Hey, Snead, you and Polski
come over here!"

A slim, quick youth started toward the sergeants. Then
he stopped, turned around, took Polski by the arm, and led
the big bearlike soldier to the house.

"Stan," Bull Cotton said, "how'd you like to guard prisoners for a while?"

Stan Polski's round blue eyes were blank. His beard-
stubbled face looked dead.

"How about it, Stan?"

"P-p-prisoners? You said prisoners, Bull?"

"Yeah. I'm pulling the platoon out of here, but I need a good man to hold down those POWs. All you have to do is stay in the house with them and see they don't get away. Okay, Stan?"

A ripple of emotion crossed the mirrorlike blue eyes. It might be fear, hope, or guilt. Pyotr couldn't tell.

"But—I'm a BAR man, Bull." Polski's loose lips began to twitch. "A BAR man don't guard prisoners, Bull. A BAR man—"

"You're tired, Stan. You don't know how tired. All I'm asking is, will you take it easy for a while?"

Polski's lips jerked crazily. He raised a bear-sized paw to hide his mouth. His voice filtered through the shaking fingers, hoarse and muffled.

"D-d-does it show that bad, Bull?"

Bull nodded.

"You mean I got combat exhaustion?"

Again Bull nodded.

Polski lowered his hand. His mouth had stopped twitching, but now tears were streaming from his eyes. They ran down his hollow cheeks and under his chin, but he didn't seem to know he was crying. Schmidt coughed loudly and drew the young soldier named Snead aside. Norton mumbled something and walked toward his own squad. Pyotr's eyes watered. It hurt, watching a grown man cry.

But then Polski's sightless blue eyes snapped awake. He touched his wet face and looked astonished.

"I—I guess you want my BAR, huh, Bull?"

"You left it standing against the garden wall, Stan. Snead can get it himself."

"Snead! Why, that skinny kid couldn't—"

"He'll never be as good as you are, Stan, but he'll have to do for now. When you get to feeling better you and him can swap around again."

"That's a promise, Bull?"

"That's a promise, Stan."

After that, it was easy. Polski took off his bulky ammunition belt and handed it to Bull. Snead came back from the garden wall carrying a BAR and a rifle, and the transfer of weapons was made. Pyotr watched Snead. The youth seemed very proud of his new role in the first squad.

"Take care of that M-1," Snead said to Polski. "I got it zeroed in perfect."

Polski gripped the rifle as if he meant to break it—possibly over Snead's head. Snead stepped back a pace.

"Aw, Stan, I was only—"

"Listen, you scrawny yardbird, you say one more word and I'll fracture every bone in your goldbricking head!"

Bull Cotton laughed.

"Lightest case of combat exhaustion I ever saw," he said. "Now let's put this show on the road."

He began shouting orders. Tubby Schmidt led his little band toward the embankment, where Norton's men were gathering wounded. Within ten minutes the last German, wounded or otherwise, had disappeared into the house, and the last GI had straggled down from the second floor. Some of the Americans stood idle, smoking and talking. Some sat on their helmets and drooped tiredly. The third platoon looked like a railroad track gang after a hard day driving spikes.

Bull Cotton smiled sweetly at his men.

"You-all rested your itty-bitty bones?" he inquired.

Some men cursed. Some groaned. Others just dropped their cigarettes in the snow and waited.

"Third platoon—fall in!"

Polski fell in at the end of Tubby Schmidt's squad. Pyotr fell in beside him.

"Polski and Russky, get inside!"

"But sergeant," Pyotr said, "can't I come with you?"

"No dice, Russky. You got prisoners to guard, remember?"

Pyotr frowned. He heard someone snicker, and felt hot in the face.

"No," he said, "I *don't* remember. You didn't tell me—"

"Clean the wax out of your ears, boy. You can take Grinstead's rifle—it's leaning against the wall over yonder—and Polski will teach you how to shoot it. Right, Stan?"

Polski said nothing.

"Polski!"

"Huh?"

"I said you're going to teach the kid how to shoot, Stan. No, no, not Snead. The one standing next to you, on your left. His name's Russky. He's going to bring you a rifle and you're going to teach him how to shoot it. You got that, Stan?"

"Yeah, sarge."

"Then go inside the house and guard prisoners, Stan."

Polski plodded toward the house.

"Go get Grinstead's rifle, Russky."

Pyotr stood his ground.

"Russky, go get that rifle like I told you!"

An order was an order and Pyotr had to obey it. But he wanted to say something to show Bull Cotton how he felt. Something American. Oh, yes. Bud Parente had said it this morning, after he stepped on a man's foot and the man had sworn at him.

"Nuts to you," he mumbled.

"What's that, Russky?"

"Nuts to you!" Pyotr snarled. "Clean the lead out of your head and you'll hear better!"

He streaked for the wall. It was chest-high. He slapped his hands on top of it and vaulted over. He fell in a heap and just lay there, resting. If Bull Cotton wanted to catch him, Bull Cotton would catch him, and that was that.

On the other side of the wall, Bull Cotton laughed. There

was a long silence, an order, and the sound of men marching out of step. There they went, a gallant band of brothers led by a petty tyrant. A bully. Well, he *acted* like a bully, didn't he?

Sometimes. When he wasn't acting like a hero.

Pyotr stood up. The last of the third platoon was going over the little rise that blocked his view of the battle for the town. He waved, but nobody saw him. Beyond the rise, automatic weapons rattled endlessly, but they sounded far away. He turned his head and looked at Grinstead's rifle. He picked it up. The weight of the M-1 surprised him. It must be powerful. This heavy wooden stock and hand guard were made to absorb shock. The rifle had a blade front sight and a ring rear sight. Hmmm.

He raised the rifle to his shoulder, steadied himself against the drag of the long barrel, and aimed at a stone.

Ah! A perfect sight picture!

Bud had said that the M-1 was gas-operated, clip-fed and semi-automatic. Compared to the light, single-shot rifle he had carried when he went hunting with his father, it was a portable cannon. Cautiously he drew back the oddly shaped bolt handle. It was a small, curved thing that didn't even look like a bolt handle, and it resisted. He pulled harder with his index finger. The bolt drew back just enough for him to see the gleam of a steel-jacketed bullet. Well, it was loaded, anyway. Perhaps he really should go inside and let Polski show him the rest. Polski didn't want to, of course, but Bull had given an order and Polski would have to do it.

Pyotr looked over the wall at the house.

Someone was standing in the doorway.

He stared at the man, gasped, and dropped to his knees. The man in the doorway was the German oberleutnant, and the oberleutnant was carrying the Professor's carbine!

The image stayed with Pyotr as he knelt in the snow.

The German officer had been glancing hurriedly from right to left, and that meant he was checking for outside guards. And if he was checking for outside guards, that meant he had a few seconds to waste. And if he had any time at all to waste, that meant he had already killed . . .

"Oh, God," Pyotr whispered, "please don't let them be dead."

Behind his closed eyes, his mind went to work.

Bud had said, this morning in the darkness, that the M-1 had a safety catch inside the trigger guard. Bud had just been talking to ease the tension of waiting, but Pyotr remembered that—or did he? Maybe Bud had said the opposite. He opened his eyes. The safety catch *was* inside the trigger guard. He pushed it forward. Now the rifle would fire. Unless he had misunderstood. If it was the other way around, he had made a mistake that would cost him his life. He pulled the safety catch. Now it was inside the trigger guard. No, he thought. Bud said *push*, not pull.

He pushed the safety catch and stood up. In the same movement he raised the rifle and aimed at the doorway. The doorway was empty. The German officer, half-crouched, was gliding toward the rear of the house.

"Halt!" Pyotr shouted.

The German pivoted easily, carbine coming up, ready to fire.

Pyotr jerked the trigger. The M-1 blasted. The heavy steel butt plate slammed into his shoulder and spun him halfway around. He winked twice, as two carbine bullets pinged on top of the wall and went keening off into space.

He ducked.

A third bullet chipped the wall where his head had been.

Then the German stopped firing.

He will either escape or come and get me, Pyotr thought. If he escapes the other Germans will follow him. And if he comes to get me, what can I do?

Move, Bud Parente's voice said suddenly, inside his head. *That's what's kept me alive, kid. I never take it for granted they got me pinned down. One way or the other, I move.*

Pyotr moved quietly along the wall. Without allowing himself to think, he stood up, rifle ready, half expecting to see the German leering at him across the wall.

Instead, he saw the officer running toward the embankment. He leaned forward, bracing himself for the blow of the rifle butt. He squeezed the trigger. The M-1 rocked him back. The German was still running. He fired again, and again. The German kept on running. He fired still again, heard a clang close to his ear, and squeezed the trigger one more time. Nothing happened. The rifle would not fire. It had made that clanging noise when it ejected the spent clip, and now it was empty.

But the German was down. He was lying on his face in the snow. Just lying there, motionless.

He was dead.

Pyotr threw the rifle over the wall. He failed twice before he managed to clamber over the top and fall to the ground on the other side. He scooped up the rifle and ran toward the house. The M-1 was empty, and even if he had more ammunition he didn't know how to load it. But perhaps the Germans wouldn't know it was empty. Perhaps he could threaten them with it and hold them until help came.

But someone was blocking the doorway.

"Hello, kid," Polski said.

Polski was still carrying Snead's M-1. And smiling.

"Th-th-they didn't disarm you?" Pyotr gasped.

"Disarm me?" Polski frowned, puzzled, then went on smiling. "Heck, them krauts ain't up to disarming nobody. I was sitting there, watching them, kind of, and I heard a noise behind me. I thought about turning around, see, but then I noticed one of them wink and jerk his head. I wondered about that, but by the time I turned around he was gone. The one that snuck off, I mean."

"You mean—you mean he slipped out of the house without you even *seeing* him?"

"I guess so, sonny." Polski went on smiling, guiltily now. "I ain't quick like I used to be."

Pyotr gently pushed him aside. The German wounded lay in neat rows across the parlor, and another row ran down the hallway. The unwounded prisoners, those who were not bending over the wounded, tending them, formed a clump of curious onlookers just outside the kitchen door.

"Get back inside," Polski said.

The Germans obeyed quickly.

Pyotr clamped his hands over his throbbing temples and tried to think. As nearly as he could fit the pieces together, Polski had been guarding these prisoners in the kitchen when the officer had come creeping up the cellar stairs. The officer could have killed Polski, but one of his own men had signaled him to keep on going behind Polski's back. So Polski was alive. But . . .

The Professor!

Halfway down the cellar stairs, Pyotr stopped abruptly. The Professor was sitting on the floor, massaging the base of his skull. Pyotr sat down on the bottom step and waited.

"He slugged me," the Professor said fuzzily. "Slugged me from behind while I was loosening a tourniquet on somebody's leg. Check Lopez's leg, will you, Pete?"

Pyotr got up, searched for a man with a wounded leg, and found him. The leg was bleeding badly but Pyotr tightened the tourniquet without feeling the least bit sick. He went back to the steps and sat down again.

"I killed him," he said.

The Professor looked up. "Killed who, Pete?"

"That German officer," Pyotr said. "He was getting away, Professor. I had to do it."

The Professor grunted. Then he began crawling in a circle, searching for something.

"Glasses," he muttered.

"They're lying next to Lopez's mattress," Pyotr said.

The Professor picked up the glasses, bent one templepiece into shape, and put them on. They canted crazily across his nose. He fumbled with them, twisting and bending the frame, until at last his eyes were peering owlishly through the lenses.

"Still off center," he said, "but they'll do for the present." He sighed. "I'm sorry, Pete. No normal person likes killing. But this is war, and sometimes we have to do it."

"I didn't have to do it," Pyotr said. "He was running away and I didn't have to do it. I—"

Now he felt the sensation he should have had when he tightened the tourniquet on Lopez's bleeding leg. He was deathly sick.

"You mean you wanted to kill him, Pete?"

Pyotr nodded.

"Kill who?" Polski said from the top of the stairs.

"That German officer," the Professor said. "Leave him alone, Stan. He's not feeling well."

"I ain't bothering him none," Polski said. "And besides, he didn't kill nobody."

Pyotr turned his head slowly.

"What do you mean?" he said.

"I mean—well, I heard this shooting outside, see, so I went to the parlor window. The side window, that is. I didn't see nothing, so I went to the other window. And there was this guy running away. And, well, he was a kraut so I let him have it, that's all."

"I see," the Professor said.

Then he reached out just in time to save Pyotr from falling face forward on the cellar floor.

Chapter 8

OPERATION BELLYROBBER

Pyotr gave the cookie tin one last hard rub, then carried it over to the window. The deep, square baking pan gleamed. It was so shiny that he could see his face in the bottom. He bared his teeth and growled. The heat-warped metal mirrored a lopsided, lumpy-cheeked grin.

"What you growling about, boy?"

"He's growling because he's on KP," Polski said. "You ever hear of anybody that liked KP, Bellyrobber?"

Staff Sergeant Virgil "Bellyrobber" Bass laid down his stirring spoon, wiped a greasy rag across his sweating hairless head, and glared at Technician Fifth Grade Stanley Polski.

"No," he said, "and I never heard of any self-respecting mess sergeant that liked having a broken-down BAR man palmed off on him as a cook, either."

"I didn't ask to be no cook," Polski said. "Like I told you, Cap'n Croft, he takes me aside, real confidential, and he says, 'Stan'—that's what he always calls me, see—'Stan, you need a rest. So here's what I want you to do. I want you to accept these here T-5 stripes as a token of my esteem. And then I want you to go over to that fouled-up excuse for a company kitchen and show that bald-headed—'"

"Show *me?* Why, you—"

"'—and show that bald-headed, stump-jumping hillbilly mess sergeant how a *real* soldier operates in a company kitchen. Stan,' he says, 'I'm depending on you to set a example—'"

"Example! Why, you shell-shocked, fumble-fingered Polack! You can't even boil water, and you got the nerve—"

Pyotr raised his stack of scrubbed, polished cookie tins high in the air. He let them drop. They landed on a pile of mess kits which he also had cleaned since noon, and the result sounded like a bomb going off in a boiler factory. Bellyrobber Bass and Stan Polski didn't even notice. They went right on insulting each other. He finished tidying up the kitchen and slipped out into the street.

None of the houses in this area had been struck by shells, and all were full of sleeping soldiers. Oboe Company had "hit the sack" late last night, after being pulled out of the line and marched back to this town. The men had slept until breakfast, then had slept again until noon chow, and now were sleeping once more, trying to regain their combat-drained energies.

He slopped through pools of slushy water until he came to the company CP. The guard beside the door opened his eyes, said, "Hi, Russky," yawned, and went back to sleep standing up. Pyotr opened the door and looked inside.

A dozen mummies in sleeping bags lay snoring in the parlor and he knew what to expect in the rooms beyond. He closed the door and trudged up the street.

Farther along the line of tall, narrow houses, he had to step aside for a jeep. Another jeep sped by, splashing him with slush. Both jeeps pulled up near the battalion CP. Two captains jumped out, greeted each other, then went inside. Their drivers remained at the wheel.

Pyotr strolled up casually and checked the jeeps' markings. N-112 and P-112. And there was Q-112 parked across the street. Three jeeps, and probably three captains, from three different outfits. He didn't see O-112, but Captain Croft could have walked here from the nearby Oboe CP. The colonel must have called a conference of company commanders.

They're all in there now, Pyotr thought. When they come
out, something will happen.

He coughed politely and smiled at the CP guard.

"Babe," he said.

"Huh?"

"Babe," Pyotr repeated. "Now you are supposed to say
'Ruth' and let me pass."

"Oh, am I!" the guard said. "Listen, buster—"

One of the jeep drivers laughed. "This is the Russian DP
kid Oboe Company picked up," he said. "He's okay, Smitty.
He's a sort of mascot."

"Well, mascot or not, he shouldn't be wandering around
town giving the password away. Suppose he gave it to a spy
or something. Suppose—"

"You are not a spy or something," Pyotr said. "You are a
duly accredited sentry at the battalion command post. I
have supplied the password correctly. Now may I enter the
building?"

The guard scowled. The jeep driver laughed again.

"What do you want in the CP, Russky?"

"I wish to speak to Pfc. Lindner."

"Pfc. who?"

"He is known as the Professor."

This time the guard laughed.

"What do you want to see the Professor about, kid?"

"It is—ah—a personal matter."

"Uh-huh. Well, remember, they're pretty busy in there
right now, so you just tell the Professor what you got to tell
him and clear out. He hasn't got time—"

Pyotr didn't hear the last words. He was inside the CP.
To the left, voices rumbled behind closed parlor doors. The
conference, he thought, and went down the hall. In the dining room he saw a switchboard operator plugging in calls,
two radio men winding up an SCR-280, a sergeant talking
into a field phone, clerks writing at the table, several run-

ners sitting on the floor, smoking and waiting. Message center, he thought, and kept on going. At the kitchen door he stopped. The Professor and a staff sergeant were sitting at opposite ends of the oilcloth-covered table, each bending over a map, working fast with tracing paper and colored pencils. Between them sat a tall, burly first lieutenant with crinkly, carrot-red hair and a snub nose surrounded by an army of freckles.

The officer winked at Pyotr.

"Hi, Russky-o. How's the boy?"

"I am in excellent health, thank you, sir. Whom have I the honor of addressing?"

For some reason the officer burst into laughter. The staff sergeant chuckled but continued working. The Professor laid down his pencil and beamed.

"Didn't I tell you, sir?" he asked the officer.

"You didn't exaggerate, Professor."

"There's no one else in the world like him," the Professor said, and turned to Pyotr. "Pete, this is our battalion intelligence officer, Lieutenant Gannon—better known to the foxhole fraternity as Greasegun Gannon."

A thick-bellied, all-metal submachine gun hung from the redheaded officer's shoulder. It looked like the "gun" used to grease automobiles, so the American GIs called it a greasegun. Pyotr knew that Lieutenant Gannon had once been the leader of a famous special raiding unit, and this was his favorite weapon. He studied Greasegun Gannon, searching for signs of great daring. All he saw was red hair, merry blue eyes, snub nose, and freckles, freckles, freckles.

"Think you'll know me next time you see me, young fellow me lad?"

Pyotr blushed.

"I'm sorry, sir. Was I staring?"

"You were, indeed, Russky-o."

"Well, you see, sir, I have read quite a bit about the inhabitants of the British Isles—"

"I don't inhabit the British Isles. I'm a hundred per cent Irish-American from Boston."

"Oh, I knew you were Irish, sir."

"You did? How?"

"Well, you see, sir, I have read about the great wave of Irish immigration to America—"

"I am not a great wave of Irish immigration," Greasegun Gannon said, "and I demand to know why you're still staring."

Pyotr tore his eyes away from the fascinating freckles.

"Sir," he said honestly, "it is just that I never dreamed that an Irishman would look so *Irish!*"

Greasegun Gannon's face turned purple, between freckles. He threw his head back and wheezed. Pyotr thought he was having an asthma attack, but then his laughter exploded with the force of a hand grenade. He pounded the table, stomped his feet, rattled dishes on the shelves, and trumpeted like a wild elephant. Finally he ran out of breath.

"I take it, sir," Pyotr said, "that a sense of humor is one of the great Irish virtues?"

Greasegun Gannon looked astonished.

"The Irish have no virtues," he said. "It is the secret of our great charm."

Pyotr tried to keep his face straight, but it didn't work. He grinned at Greasegun Gannon, and the answering twinkle in the merry blue eyes made him feel fine. He and Greasegun Gannon sat in companionable silence while the Professor and the intelligence sergeant finished their tracing. Then Greasegun Gannon gathered the papers together and stood up.

"Spiro," he said, "we'll drop these overlays off at message center and then take a little jeep ride to regiment. Profes-

sor, you're in charge until we get back." He winked at
Pyotr. "See you later, Russky-o."

He went out, followed by Staff Sergeant Spiro.

"Well," the Professor said, "how do you like him?"

"He is a most remarkable man," Pyotr said. "Soldiering
with him must be quite lively."

"Lively isn't the word for it," the Professor said. "I'm
practically night-blind. I have a lousy sense of direction.
I've gotten lost twice on contact patrols. The night you and
I met I had lost my way to the battalion OP, and if Bull
Cotton's platoon hadn't picked me up I'd probably be a
German prisoner today." He smiled his slow, sad smile.
"I'm the world's worst scout and observer, but Greasegun
refuses to believe it. He keeps me busy—getting lost."

Pyotr laughed, but secretly he wished the Professor
would start thinking better of himself.

"Perhaps," he said, "Lieutenant Gannon realizes that
you have the one big thing the intelligence section needs
most—intelligence itself."

The Professor's thin face reddened. "Why, Pete," he said,
and scowled, embarrassed. "Quit buttering me up, boy.
Anyway, you didn't come here to talk about us Quiz Kids.
You want to know what comes next for you, right?"

Pyotr nodded.

"I saw Captain Croft this morning, Pete, and he was very
much interested in your case. In fact, he already knew a
lot because Bull Cotton bent his ear last night. The catch
is, he simply hasn't got the time to do anything about you
now. We're going into the attack again—I'm sure you've
seen the signs—and when it's over Captain Croft will do all
he can to help you. Meanwhile you're eating good chow
and sleeping in a feather bed. As long as we stay in the
Colmar Pocket you're taken care of."

"But if the 28th Division is ordered elsewhere I'll be left
behind?"

"Maybe not, Pete. Maybe—" The Professor shrugged and spread his hands wide, palms up. "Listen, boy, all any of us can do is stick with the outfit and hope to stay alive."

Pyotr sighed heavily. But he mustn't think only of his own troubles. That was selfish.

"When the attack starts, Professor, you'll go forward with the OP party as usual?"

Again the Professor shrugged and spread his hands. It was a gesture his grandfather must have brought to America from some little Jewish village in Poland. It seemed to say, "Naturally I'll go forward, and the worst is bound to happen, but what else can I do?" Yet the Professor's brown eyes were steady behind the owl-like steel rims of his glasses. He would stick with the outfit beyond hope of staying alive.

Pyotr wished he could say good-by in the warm, sentimental Russian fashion, but the Americans always tried to hide what they felt. He stood up briskly.

"Well, take it easy, Prof," he said. "Don't go buckin' for no wooden overcoat."

The Professor shook his head in amazement.

"Your gift for languages will make you rich yet, Pete. So long. See you later."

Outside again, Pyotr decided that a good slide on the river ice was what he needed to ease his mind. But at the edge of town he found a free-flowing stream. The center ice had melted and the rest was too rotten for safety. A pontoon bridge spanned the river, and a muddy road led across the valley to rocky foothills that might be fun climbing. But beside the road there stood a small T-shaped sign which the Germans had put up to warn their own troops, and then had forgotten to take down before the Americans came. The sign said *"Achtung! Minen!"*—"Attention! Mines!" —and if he took just one careless step off the road into that mine field, he would never see tomorrow.

Glumly he walked back toward the kitchen. As he neared the house a six-by-six supply truck rumbled away from the front door. He stepped inside and saw four men staring at a big pile of boxes. Bellyrobber Bass and Stan Polski looked angry, but not with each other. Jenkins and Poggi, the cooks who had been off duty sleeping, just looked disgusted.

"May I ask what is wrong?" Pyotr said.

"Wrong?" Bellyrobber swatted his bald head. "He wants to know what's wrong!"

Pyotr turned to Stan Polski.

"Read what's on them boxes," Stan said.

"Flour, sugar, cherries," Pyotr read aloud. He brightened. "Are we going to bake cherry pies?"

"We *was* going to," Stan said. "The way we figured it, if regiment delivered the makings this morning, we could bake the pies this afternoon and serve them to the company for supper. But then the orders come through to attack, and the supplies didn't arrive 'til ten minutes ago. That means no pie tonight. It means poor old Oboe Company will move out and live on cold K rations for maybe five-ten days."

Bellyrobber Bass began to swear. He was an old Regular who had seen much foreign service, and he could speak pidgin French, Spanish, Tagalog, and Cantonese as well as hillbilly English. He swore for five minutes in five languages without repeating himself, and then he stopped.

"Sergeant," Pyotr said, "I have been thinking."

"Well, ain't that nice," Bellyrobber said.

"This sort of thing has happened before, has it not?"

"Yeah. Too many times before."

"What did you do, sergeant?"

"Do? Well, if there wasn't too much stuff for the kitchen truck to hold, we hung onto it 'til we caught up with the outfit. Then, if they was in a nice quiet defense position, we'd feed 'em hot chow 'til"—Bellyrobber groaned—"'til Oboe had to move out sudden again and we was left with another useless batch of supplies on our hands."

"I see. And what did you do if the kitchen truck could not carry the supplies?"

"Oh, we'd give 'em to the frog civilians, if there was any around."

"And if there were none around?"

"We'd have to dump the stuff, that's all."

Pyotr gritted his teeth. All over Europe, people were hungry. Throwing away food was criminal. He held back his anger and tried to speak calmly.

"Sergeant Bass, is there no way we can carry cherry pie to the troops tonight?"

Bellyrobber Bass looked as if he might lose his temper again, but he didn't.

"Son," he said, "I got the poop from the CP an hour ago. This here is going to be a night attack. Oboe's objective is seven miles from town. The road's only good for about two-three miles, and after that it's cross-country all the way. The trails ain't marked. We'd have to go by compass, lugging marmite cans that'd weigh a ton before we topped the first hill. And there ain't nothing but hills out there, boy. Why, we'd be lucky if we got halfway to Oboe Company. We'd end up dumping all that pie in the middle of nowhere. . . ."

Bellyrobber's nasal drawl trailed off, because Pyotr had turned away from him and walked to the window. Pyotr gazed sightlessly into the darkening street until he felt a hand on his shoulder. From the size of the hand, he knew it belonged to Stan Polski.

"I am all right, Stan," he said.

"If you're all right," Stan said, "how come you sound like you want to bawl?"

"Bawl?" Pyotr said. "I assure you—" He stopped because his choked voice gave him away.

There was a wordless pause. Stan's hand stayed on Pyotr's shoulder. Then Chuck Jenkins spoke.

"Look, Bellyrobber, I know it sounds crazy, but why don't we give it a whirl?"

"Just because a stray DP kid wants us to? You call that a reason?"

"I'm willing to try," Mario Poggi broke in suddenly. "It wouldn't hurt to try, Bellyrobber."

"You got frostbit feet, Mario. You wouldn't last a mile and you know it."

"But—"

"I said you're a frostbite case!" Bellyrobber screeched. "That's why Cap'n Croft took you out of the line and put you in the kitchen. You want to end up in a hospital with your feet cut plumb off?"

"I could drive the jeep," Mario said.

"Sure you could," Chuck Jenkins said. "And there's nothing wrong with the rest of our feet, Bellyrobber."

"It's what's wrong with your heads that bothers me," Bellyrobber said. "Ain't you got no sense at all?"

"I sure do," Chuck said. "Now look. You mentioned lugging marmite cans. That would keep the pies warm, sure. But suppose we left them in the cookie tins we baked them in. They'd get cold, but think of the weight we'd save. And after the carry we could warm them up with Coleman stoves." Jenkins giggled, shrill with excitement. "How about it, Bellyrobber?"

"I'm not a-going to do it, Chuck. That's final."

Stan Polski's hand squeezed Pyotr's shoulder.

"Look, Bellyrobber," he said, "I don't like to talk about morale. It sounds phony. But try to see this thing like a man on straight line duty would. You're up there in a foxhole, freezing. You got to hang on 'til morning and you don't think you'll make it. And then some old beat-up cook comes along and sticks a piece of hot cherry pie in your face. He's only a rear-echelon has-been, but he knows how you feel, and he's practically broke his back trying to prove he's a real buddy. So when that old cook hands you that slab of pie, it *means* something. You—"

Bellyrobber slapped at thin air, as if he were swatting a leftover summer fly.

"Quit sweet-talking me," he said. "I used to be a squad leader in the hedgerows. I know as much about morale as anybody. But this here mountain climbing caper hasn't got nothing to do with morale. It ain't practical. I don't want no part of it."

"Okay, then, if you don't want to go, don't go. But how about letting the rest of us go?"

"Listen, Polski, you been shooting your mouth off all day but you ain't fooling me none. You got combat exhaustion, that's what you got. Suppose you make it to Oboe. You're strong as an ox and twict as dumb and you just might make it. But how about them mortars, Polski? And them eighty-eights. How you going to act when that stuff starts coming in, loudmouth?"

Stan Polski sighed.

"I don't know," he said humbly. "I'll just have to see when I get there."

"Getting there empty-handed seems like an awful waste of time to me." Bellyrobber cackled wickedly. "Who's going to bake them pies if I don't?"

"I will," Chuck Jenkins said. "I'm not any beat-up line doggie that's in the kitchen for a rest. I'm a trained cook and baker. I'll bake those pies, Bellyrobber."

"And what if I say nobody bakes no pies?"

The cooks said nothing. There was nothing they could say. Stan Polski's giant paw left Pyotr's shoulder. He was alone now, and beaten. And because he was alone and beaten, he turned around and faced Bellyrobber Bass.

"Congratulations on your victory, sergeant."

"Huh?"

"You have just defeated Oboe Company," Pyotr said.

Bellyrobber Bass went red from his shirt collar to the top of his bald head. He pointed a bony finger at Pyotr.

"Boy," he said, "you started this. You got no business here, but you started it. Why?"

Pyotr trembled inwardly, but he did not lower his eyes.

"Once I had a home and a family," he said. "Now I have only this outfit. I think of the outfit as my home, and the men in it as my brothers. It is as simple as that, Sergeant Bass."

Bellyrobber's Adam's apple rose and fell twice in his long, leathery neck.

"Well, I'll be durned," he said.

Stan Polski nudged Pyotr with his elbow.

"Bellyrobber," he said, "I been thinking."

"You been *what?*"

"Thinking. A minute ago you said you used to be a squad leader. Now you're back in the kitchen. Why did they send you back here, Bellyrobber?"

"Why, the medics said there was something wrong with my inside ear. A shell landed right next to my hole, see, and after that I kept getting sort of falling-down dizzy spells—" Suddenly Bellyrobber thrust his naked head forward like an angry turkey gobbler about to attack. "Polski, are you telling me I got combat exhaustion too?"

"I guess I am," Stan said sadly. "It sounds better than saying you're scared to carry pie up front and scareder still of staying home alone."

Up the street, near the CP, a whistle blew. Bellyrobber wiped his shiny sweating head with his favorite greasy rag. And then he began to swear.

"That was chow call," Chuck Jenkins said.

Bellyrobber Bass went right on swearing.

Chuck snorted in disgust.

"All right, guys," he said. "Let's dish it out."

The men formed a line in the street. Their steel cups and mess kits clinked and rattled as they drifted through the cobblestoned alleyway. They stopped at the four serving stations near the kitchen door and then scattered in the snow-dappled garden. Some sat on their helmets in the snow, placing their mess kits on the ground. Some entered the tool shed at the rear of the garden, where they could sit on boxes and boards. And some lined up along the garden wall, resting their mess kits on top of the flat stones. They ate fast and talked little. This night Oboe Company would go into the attack, and Oboe's riflemen did not feel like talking.

Now and then someone would exchange greetings with Pyotr. Bull Cotton did, very cheerful on the surface, and so did Tubby Schmidt and a few others. But what could he say to line-duty men? He crouched beside his serving pot, dumping dehydrated mashed potatoes into the yawning mess kits, pouring good brown gravy over the lumpy hills of potatoes, wishing he might say something that would have meaning to these young men, his brothers, but never finding the words.

One teen-age rifleman leaned over in a corner of the wall and vomited up all that he had eaten. But the chowhound majority downed second helpings, scraped the leavings into the garbage can, tossed their mess kits into a jumbled pile, and walked out into the street loosening their belts.

Soon the garden was empty, and the cleanup began. All of the mess kits had to be washed, and this was Pyotr's job. First, scrubbing in hot soapy water. Second, rinsing in clear boiling water. Third, tumble-drying the kits in an old mattress cover, and stacking them away in the kit chest. After that, pots and pans. Pyotr worked fast and hard. An hour passed. Another hour. And then, out in the street, boots sloshed through snowy slush. Metal gear clinked. There was a creaking of leather and web equipment, an occasional murmur of voices, as the greatest company of dogface soldiers in the world marched off into the bitter February night. And after that there was no sound beyond the kitchen, no sound except the swish of soapy brushes against cooking utensils, and the brief mumble of cooks' voices as they swapped work-talk.

At last it was over.

Pyotr went to the rear door. He sat down on the back steps. He sat with his elbows on his knees, face buried in his hands, and he tried not to think.

After a while he heard footsteps behind him.

"Stan?" he said.

The toe of a combat boot dug into his rump. He turned his head and looked upward.

It was Bellyrobber Bass.

"Get up off your lazy butt, boy," Bellyrobber Bass said. "We got cherry pie to bake."

Chapter 9

HI JOLLY AND THE MAGIC MULES

Staff Sergeant Nick Spiro had keen black eyes and clever black eyebrows which he could raise into devil's peaks whenever he felt like it. He felt like it now.

"An urgent message from Bellyrobber?" he said. "Sit down and catch your breath while I read it."

Still puffing from his run to the battalion CP, Pyotr dropped into a chair. Except for the intelligence sergeant and a few message center men, the house was deserted. The rest of Headquarters Company had gone ahead to set up a forward CP, and soon this rear CP would cease to exist. Bellyrobber had sent Pyotr on his run just in time.

"So Bellyrobber wants a luminous-dial compass and an overlay of the routes to Oboe," Sergeant Spiro said. "Can you tell me what this is all about?"

Pyotr hesitated. But perhaps the intelligence sergeant had a right to know.

"Sergeant Bass plans to carry hot cherry pie right up to the foxholes," he said with a touch of pride.

Nick Spiro's eyebrows steepled again.

"Will wonders never cease," he said. "Well, if Bellyrobber is crazy enough to try it, I'll help him. Wait a minute and I'll make the overlay."

"Could you make two overlays, sergeant?"

"Two overlays? Why?"

"Oh, just in case," Pyotr said. "Sergeant Bass thought the carrying party might become separated or something of the sort."

"Huh!" Nick Spiro said, but he traced two overlays from his map and handed them to Pyotr.

"Now," he said, "the LD compass."

"Two compasses, please, sergeant."

Sergeant Spiro frowned. But if the carrying party did become separated, they would need two compasses as well as two overlays. He fished the compasses out of a musette bag and pushed them across the table.

"There you are," he said. "Give my regards to Bellyrobber and tell him I wish him the best of luck."

"Wilco," Pyotr said. "Roger and out."

Nick Spiro laughed, because this bright foreign youngster had picked up GI radio code so fast. Pyotr laughed also, but for a different reason.

Back in the company kitchen, he gave one compass and one overlay to Bellyrobber Bass. The other set stayed in his jacket pocket. "Where is Mario?" he asked innocently.

"He goofed off somewheres," Bellyrobber said. "He ain't needed 'til the pies is done."

Pyotr sat down at the table with Bellyrobber, Stan Polski, and Chuck Jenkins. Ranged against the brick back wall, three M-1937 field stoves were busy baking pies. Each stove had three burner units, so it could bake three pies at once. Three stoves, times three pies each, equaled nine pies. And nine pies, baked in $2\frac{1}{2}' \times 2\frac{1}{2}'$ cookie tins, would furnish three hundred pieces for Oboe Company. Bellyrobber Bass didn't believe in doing things by halves.

"Sure, the outfit's way under strength," he had said earlier. "So what? Let's bake up every last bit of these dad-blamed supplies. Then every dog soldier out there will get two-three helpings—if we can carry the load, that is."

Could three cooks carry so much weight over those cruel frozen hills? Pyotr doubted it, and this gave him courage for one last try at persuasion. When Mario Poggi came back into the kitchen, he saw his chance.

"Welcome back, Mario," he said. "Do they fit?"

"They sure do," Mario said happily. "There was about ten pair I could choose from."

"Ten pair of what?" Bellyrobber growled.

"Shoepacs," Pyotr said. "See, Mario's wearing shoepacs now, instead of combat boots. I'll bet you could walk twenty miles in those shoepacs, Mario."

"I sure could," Mario said. "They're so soft and easy on the feet—"

"And just right for winter weather," Pyotr said.

"Yeah. If I'd of wore them in the Bulge I wouldn't of got frostbit at all."

"Of course not," Pyotr said. "They're made of rubber up to the ankles, so your feet can't get wet. And those felt inner boots should keep anybody's feet warm. They look so comfortable, Mario. It's a shame that you are not coming with us tonight."

"Yeah!" Mario said. "Look, Bellyrobber—"

"No!" Bellyrobber roared. "For the hundredth time, no! You're driving the jeep and that's all you're going to do, Poggi. And as for you"—he whirled on Pyotr—"you're not going nowhere." Bellyrobber thumped the table with his fist. "I never seen such a stubborn young one. Why don't you settle for a nice warm place to sleep and keep your fool mouth shut?"

Pyotr kept his fool mouth shut for five minutes. When he opened it again he whispered to Mario:

"Where did you get those shoepacs? Battalion supply?"

"Uh-uh. They'd pulled out already. I bummed these from the medics at the aid station."

"Medics? What are they doing with extra shoepacs?"

"They take them off the wounded. There's always a bunch of weapons and uniforms and equipment lying around the aid station." Mario eyed Pyotr closely. "Are you sure I'll be needing these shoepacs tonight?"

"Dead sure, Mario."

Pyotr patted the pocket where he had hidden the compass and overlay. Mario grinned. Pyotr leaned forward and stared at the three hard-working stoves.

Hurry up and do your duty, he told them sternly.

Half an hour later, Bellyrobber stepped over to the nearest stove and tested three pies.

"Done," he said. "Now it's a job for us poor mules."

But the poor mules had a plan:

They piled eight cookie tins into two stacks, four tins in each stack. ("This here ninth pie ruins the balance," Bellyrobber said. "We'll leave it for a homecoming snack.")

They wrapped warm blankets around the stacks of cookie tins, then lashed thick tarpaulins over the blankets. (But they did not cover the D-rings, or metal pick-up handles of the tins.)

They ran strong ropes through the D-rings, then tied the ends of the ropes to three "butterflies," or canvas bib-yokes ordinarily used to carry mortar ammunition. Thus, when the three human mules put on their yokes, the two stacks of cookie tins would hang between them, "divvying up the load equal, sort of," as Bellyrobber described it. Stan, ordered to wear the middle yoke, complained that he seemed to be a little more equal than the other mules, but Bellyrobber just told him to stop griping.

When the strange contraption was ready, the crew dragged it outside and stowed it in the jeep trailer. Mario took the wheel of the jeep. Bellyrobber slid into the front seat beside him. Stan and Chuck occupied the rear seat —and Pyotr hopped into the trailer with the pies.

"Get back in that kitchen, boy!"

"Aw, sarge," Mario said, "let him come a ways with us. He'll be company for me on the drive back."

Bellyrobber started to swear, but cut it short.

"Oh, well, what's the difference," he said. "Let's go."

And off they went.

Three miles down the road, Mario braked the jeep.

"End of the line, sarge."

Bellyrobber, Stan and Chuck hauled their mule harness out of the trailer. They poked their heads through the holes in the butterfly yokes and stood up. Stan, the middle mule, bore half the weight of two stacks of cookie tins, but Bellyrobber and Chuck did all the groaning.

"We'll never make it," Bellyrobber said, and stepped off into the darkness.

Pyotr joined Mario in the front seat of the jeep.

"We had better study our overlay," he said.

Mario pulled a shelter half from under his seat. He threw it over himself and Pyotr to form a blackout tent. Then he used his flashlight to examine the overlay.

"Gee, this is as good as a map, Russky. Let's see, now—where are we?"

"Here," Pyotr said, pointing. "From here, the road runs in a corkscrew curve for about two miles. It is supposed to be interdicted—"

"Inter-what?"

"Interdicted. Meaning under enemy fire and not usable by us. But I have not heard any shells falling in this area for hours. Why don't we take a chance and drive ahead to this point?" He made an X with a stub of pencil.

"Why there, Russky?"

"Because there the trail Sergeant Bass is following comes down out of the hills and almost joins the road."

"So we park the jeep and wait on the trail for Bellyrobber?"

"Exactly," Pyotr said.

Mario drove fast. He made a tight U-turn and parked the jeep in the ditch.

"So far, so good," Pyotr said.

And, far to the east, the telltale whistling began.

"Hit the dirt!" Mario said.

He threw himself out of the jeep. Pyotr vaulted over the steering wheel and landed on top of him. Mario's yowl of pain sounded like the faint meow of a kitten in a hurricane. The incoming shells screeched louder, louder, louder, and burst less than fifty yards up the road.

After three more wailing, screaming, thunderous flights of shells, the German artillery shifted its sights about a thousand yards to the west.

Mario sat up, breathing hard.

"I am sorry," Pyotr said. "It was my idea."

"I bought it, didn't I?" Mario said. "Anyways, we can't drive back to town through that shellfire. We got to find Bellyrobber's trail, Russky."

Pyotr felt wobbly, but he followed Mario off the road and up a steep slope. Mario kept saying, "Pine trees ahead, watch it," and "Big rock ahead, swing left." Pyotr bumped into some trees. He used others to pull himself upward. Once, stopped by a deep ravine, he paused long enough to check his compass. He said, "Mario, I think we're drifting too far left."

Mario grunted and swung right. They went on like that, yard by yard, foot by foot, until Pyotr's arms and legs trembled with strain. And then Mario said, "Whoa, Russky. Wait while I do some scouting."

Pyotr heard Mario's feet sliding cautiously forward.

"Yeah, this is it, Russky. Crest of the hill. Now she ought to slope down 'til she hits that trail."

Hurrying to catch up, Pyotr slipped. He clutched at the slim trunk of a young pine tree, and the tree seemed to dodge out of his way. He went rolling downhill until another tree stopped him. He was still lying in the snow when Mario came.

"Hurt bad?" Mario said.

"No," Pyotr said. "Luckily I struck the tree with my hip instead of my head."

"With the kind of head you got, I ain't so sure," Mario said. "Get up and act sensible for a change."

Pyotr obeyed meekly. Halfway down the hill they came to a wide, level shelf.

"This must be the trail," Mario said. "Let's take a load off our feet and wait."

They waited, and they waited, slowly freezing to death. Then Pyotr heard the slow, heavy crunch, crunch, crunch of boots on crusted snow.

"We're in for it now," Mario whispered.

Pyotr almost jumped out of his skin.

"You mean—a German patrol?"

"Could be," Mario said. "They got patrols all over. But it's Bellyrobber I'm really scared of."

Pyotr was worse than scared. In a moment Mario would call "Halt!" and heaven only knew what would happen next.

But Mario fooled him. In a voice of solid brass, Mario yelled: "Hey, Bellyrobber!"

A few yards down the trail, there was a great thumping crash as three cooks and two stacks of cookie tins hit the dirt together. Then the swearing began.

"Come on," Mario said to Pyotr. "We're in for it now."

But by the time they reached Bellyrobber, he had sworn himself out. "You boys sure gave us a scare," he said mildly. "We was looking for an excuse to lay down and you really obliged us."

Mario said, "You real pooped, sarge?"

"Pooped ain't the word for it, Mario. We're licked. This was a fool stunt to begin with. We're just a bunch of rear-echelon has-beens that had to prove we wasn't, and I'm the worst fool of the lot." He sighed. "I never could stand being called chicken."

"Would it help if we reduced the load?" Pyotr said guilt-ily.

"Nope. Not even if we cut the load in half. These hills is just too blamed steep."

Pyotr sat down beside him.

"Mario and I thought of a funny thing to say when we surprised you on the trail, Sergeant Bass. We were going to say, 'Could you use a pair of Coleman stoves, gentlemen?' You see, we knew you were bound to forget something, and we guessed it would be the little stoves."

"By golly," Bellyrobber said, "we did forget them!"

"So did we," Pyotr said dully. "We left them in the jeep."

Bellyrobber laughed. So did Stan and Chuck and Mario. But Pyotr felt miserable, and somehow Bellyrobber sensed his mood.

"Don't take on about it, son," he said. "Leastways we can count on a free ride back to town. Where did you park the jeep, Mario?"

"By the road, sarge. It ain't far. But the catch is—" Mario burst out laughing again.

"The catch is," Pyotr said bitterly, "the Germans are shelling the road. We had to abandon the jeep and it prob-ably will be stolen. So far, I have cost Oboe Company one jeep and eight cherry pies."

He walked away, then. He could not stand jokes about a matter which was, to him, deadly serious. He wanted to be alone for a while.

As he walked, he blamed himself for everything. He had pampered himself, made others suffer because of a con-ceited, falsely sentimental, self-important whim. From now on . . .

He stopped. He stood in the middle of the trail, listening. But now all he heard was the blood pounding in his ears.

He dropped to his knees, scooped away snow, put an ear to the bare ground. He got up again, whirled around, and

raced back up the trail, reckless in his haste. He found the
kitchen crew exactly where he had left them. They were
too exhausted to move.

"Sergeant Bass," he said, "there is a German patrol coming up the trail!"

Bellyrobber whistled thoughtfully through his teeth.

"Let's go down the trail a piece," he said.

"*Down* the trail!" Chuck Jenkins said. "You mean we're
heading *toward* them?"

"Correct," Bellyrobber said. "About fifty yards downtrail
there's a boulder as big as a house. I aim to hide behind
it."

Stan and Chuck stood up at the same time Bellyrobber
did. They went down the trail at a pounding dogtrot,
with Pyotr and Mario stumbling in their wake. They tore
around the boulder, lowered the cookie tins to the ground,
and eased their heads out of the butterfly yokes.

"Shall we spread out?" Chuck asked.

"Never mind the fancy tactics," Bellyrobber said. "We're
better off hanging together in a bunch. All we've got is carbines, remember." He paused. "I don't want to hear nothing
out of nobody. And don't shoot unless they come around
this here boulder."

"They will," Chuck said. "They'll see our tracks in the
snow."

"Shut up," Bellyrobber said. "In fact, quit breathing."

Pyotr stopped breathing often as he waited. Once he
noticed the luminous dial of his compass shining. The Germans could not possibly see it from the trail, but he pulled
his sleeve down to cover it. The minutes crept by, and
then his ears began to pick up sound.

Feet, he thought. So many of them. And they make
such a funny noise.

He rubbed his ears, but the sound did not change. What
odd footsteps. Hard, metallic, clopping, like the hoofs of

shod horses. He raised his head and peered at the dense black mass of the boulder as if he could see through it. And then he heard a voice.

"Driver," the voice said in weirdly accented French, "will you please keep that beast moving? Every time he stops I bump my nose against his—"

"Professor!" Pyotr yelled, and leaped to his feet.

He tripped over Mario and stepped on Stan. He rounded the boulder at a dead run. The trail was full of strange animal shapes. He collided with one, and it whinnied an angry protest.

"Mules!" he shouted. "*Real* mules!"

Rough hands seized him, but he didn't care.

"Where is the Professor?" he asked gleefully. And seconds later that familiar voice said, "Doggone it, Pete, what are *you* doing here?"

"Carrying hot cherry pie," Pyotr said.

"Why, of course," the Professor said. "How silly of me not to realize. Hot cherry pie is just the thing for a midnight picnic in the Vosges Mountains with the temperature below zero. And you're just the boy to be carrying it, too."

"I am so glad you understand," Pyotr said sweetly. "And what are you doing here, Professor? Surely you are not lost?"

"Far from it, my boy. I am guiding a Moroccan mule train through this snowy jungle."

"Naturally," Pyotr said. "I should have known. Moroccan mule train traffic in the suburbs has been simply *impossible* lately—" He gulped. These mules around him were real enough. "Professor, do you *mean* it?"

The Professor laughed and slapped him on the shoulder.

"Yes, Pete, I mean it. This Moroccan mule train is on loan from the French First Army. We need them to carry supplies over these crazy hills. The mule drivers speak Berber and French, but not English. And since I still remem-

ber some of my high school French, Greasegun Gannon
assigned me to guide this train."

"I see," Pyotr said, dazed. He squinted at the dim forms
that circled him and the Professor. "These are all Moroc-
cans?"

"That's right. They're known as *goumiers* because tradi-
tionally they carry big curved knives called *goumia*. Would
you like to meet their leader?"

"I certainly would, Professor."

"He is a talented man, Pete. Unlike the common drivers,
he speaks very good English."

Pyotr took this as a warning not to practice his very poor
French. He sighed and waited.

The Professor coughed delicately.

"Sergeant Haj Ali El Fassy," he said, "may I present Mr.
Pyotr Dmitrievich Pribylov? Mr. Pribylov is a promising
young civilian attached to the American forces."

"Enchanted!" said the man standing next to the Professor. "Any friend of our distinguished guide is a friend of
Haj Ali El Fassy!"

Even in the darkness Pyotr could tell that the Moroccan
leader was a very fat man. As for his voice, it sounded like
the croak of a lovelorn bullfrog. But his hand, though
plump, was surprisingly strong.

"I am honored, Haj Ali El Fassy," Pyotr murmured. "And
I must compliment you on arriving in the nick of time."

"Nick? What is this nick of time, *effendi?*"

Pyotr told him all about it.

"Ho-ho!" Haj Ali El Fassy laughed like a bullfrog sultan.
"Your problem—pouf!—it is nothing. I have two extra mules
in my train. Either of them can carry your precious pies
with the greatest of ease." He harrumphed majestically.
"But where are the pies, my young friend?"

"Behind that boulder," Pyotr said. "And so are the
brave cooks—I mean chefs—"

"No we ain't," Bellyrobber said. "Us brave chefs is right here handy."

The ring of *goumiers* parted to let Bellyrobber through. Stan, Chuck, and Mario squeezed in after him. The Professor introduced them all to Haj Ali El Fassy.

Haj Ali El Fassy was enchanted.

"My *goumiers* will load your valuable pies on the back of our finest mule," he assured them. "And now, gentlemen, if you will accompany me—"

He wheeled his vast bulk around and started up the trail, still talking. He seemed to be especially enchanted by Bellyrobber, and Bellyrobber by him. Full of hillbilly good humor and curious as a pack rat, Bellyrobber asked dozens of questions.

"Yes," Haj Ali explained graciously, "the coils of cloth which circle our heads are turbans, but we call them *rezzah*." And: "Yes, as you say, our pantaloons are baggy, but we like comfort. We call them *sarrouel*." And: "How did I come to be named Hi Jolly? Listen carefully, please. Haj is a title of respect accorded those of the faithful who have made the sacred pilgrimage to Mecca. Ali is my first name—"

"I get it," Bellyrobber said. "That little jaunt to Mecca makes you Sir Ollie!"

"One might say so, yes. But if you don't mind, it is properly pronounced Haj Ali."

"Okay Hi Jolly," Bellyrobber said agreeably. "But what about that fancy last name?"

"El Fassy? It is my family name. There are many of my blood in the city of Fez."

"Hmm," Bellyrobber said thoughtfully. "I bet you got more wives than you can count, huh, Hi Jolly?"

Haj Ali croaked "Harrrumph!" and did not answer that one.

The Professor, walking beside Pyotr, whispered that Mohammedan law limited the faithful to four wives at the

most, and a poorly paid sergeant in the French Moroccan
Army would be lucky to have a wife at all. Still, in Pyotr's
opinion, Haj Ali deserved a palace in paradise, with golden
stables for his mules.

He felt warm and grateful as they topped the crest of the
last icy hill. But the Professor had a surprise in store.

"We have to turn north here," he said, "and follow the
ridge-line trail to the first battalion. But the Oboe Company
CP is just across the valley down below. Think you can
make it on foot from here, Bellyrobber?"

"No! No!" Haj Ali croaked. "You defy *kismet!* Fate has
decreed that we see our honored guests safely home!"

"But Haj Ali," the Professor said, "we have to get to the
first battalion before dawn."

"If we can live only in darkness," Haj Ali said, "then we
shall die in the full light of day. *Mektub! Bismillah!* Forward, my children!"

Down the hill went Haj Ali. Down the hill went his gallant *goumiers* and his stout-hearted, nimble little pack
mules. There was no trail. The footing could not have been
more treacherous. But the pack train reached the bottom
without mishap—cooks and cookie tins included.

Straight ahead, Pyotr saw a sea of smooth snow. Haj Ali
led his train across the white expanse and called a halt at
the far end of the last field, yards short of the road. He
leaned against a small T-shaped sign and chuckled froggily.

"Gentlemen," he said, "you are almost home."

Almost, Pyotr thought.

"Haj Ali, may I look at that sign, please?"

"Certainly." Scorning enemy artillery observers, Haj Ali
pulled a flashlight out of his baggy *sarrouel*, flashed it at
the sign, and snapped it off again.

"The sign is unreadable as well as unspeakable," he said.
"It is in German."

"I read it," Pyotr said. "It said '*Achtung! Minen!*'"

"You mean we led a whole mule train across a German mine field?" the Professor said.

"We did," Pyotr said.

"The mines must be frozen tight in the ground," the Professor said wonderingly. "That's why they didn't go off. The only reason they didn't—"

"*El hamdulillah*," Haj Ali croaked.

"What does that mean, Haj Ali?"

"Praise be to Allah," Haj Ali said, plainly bored by all this fuss over nothing. "Shall we go on, gentlemen?"

On they went, over the road and through what Pyotr took to be an apple orchard. On the other side of the orchard, a sentry challenged them.

"Party!" he said.

"Pooper!" the Professor said.

"I'm supposed to let you pass now," the sentry said, "but what is that behind you—a herd of moose?"

"Just a herd of reindeer," the Professor said, and Bellyrobber chimed in.

"Where's the CP, soldier?"

"Couple of hundred yards straight ahead. But look, that other guy said reindeer—"

"Is the CP in a tent or a dugout, junior?"

"Neither one. It's in a whopping big house. But about those rein—"

"Forward, my children," Bellyrobber said. "We got a big kitchen to play around in!"

The kitchen, like the house, was large and roomy. Willing *goumiers* carried the cookie tins inside. Bellyrobber and Mario tore off tarps and blankets. Stan and Chuck pumped up two little Coleman stoves while Pyotr raided the CP for more. In the hallway he passed three runners who were on their way to tell the good news to the rifle platoons. Upstairs he spied Captain Croft sitting at a field desk.

"Well," the captain said, "look who's here!"

They had met before, on the night Oboe Company had
pulled back out of the line. There had been no time for
talk, then, but Captain Croft fascinated Pyotr. At the age of
twenty-six, Oboe's "Old Man" was a living legend. The GIs
told of a day when Tex Croft had picked up an A-6 machine gun and strolled down the main street of an enemy-
held town, cleaning snipers out of doorways and windows
"just like in a Hollywood movie." They said he looked like
Tyrone Power, a cinema actor whom Pyotr had never seen.
But he could well believe it. Captain Travis Crockett Croft
was as handsome as a storybook prince. The son of a Texas
oil tycoon, he had been a brilliant student at the Harvard
Law School when the United States entered the war. He
had volunteered, of course, and here he was now—wearing
a pearl-handled six-shooter instead of the regulation Army
automatic, and in a quick-draw holster at that.

My cowboy captain from Texas, Pyotr thought, even
though he knew Tex Croft had been a student of law.

"Good evening, sir," he said. "I am here because Sergeant
Bass very kindly brought me along."

"That isn't the way I heard it," Captain Croft said. He
gave Pyotr a light, playful punch on the shoulder. "I'll drop
down to the kitchen for a visit just as soon as I get the
chance."

"Oh, thank you, sir!"

Pyotr walked off in a daze, but he did have wits enough
left to borrow one Coleman stove from the communications
sergeant and another from the supply sergeant. When he
brought them into the kitchen, he found that the pie-serv-
ing operation was in full swing.

Bellyrobber could not permit a parade through the
kitchen, so the men stayed out in the cold. Cookie tins were
passed to them under blackout conditions, and because
the line could not be left unguarded, they had to eat in
shifts. Pyotr heard excited talk, and now and then an out-

right yelp of pleasure, but he wished he could *see* them eat.

Within an hour, the cherry pie party was over. The GIs had returned to their freezing foxholes, and the Professor was more than anxious to get the pack train moving again.

"If we just stop yakking and *go*," he said with a severe glance at Haj Ali, "we can still make it to the first battalion before dawn."

Leisurely and with great dignity, Haj Ali adjusted his tent-stripped *rezzah*, kissed Bellyrobber on both cheeks, and strode to the door.

"*El hamdulillah*," he croaked, and vanished into the night.

Alone in the kitchen, the cooks did not know what to do with themselves. Their great adventure was over, and they felt empty, without purpose.

Chuck Jenkins wandered over to the section of pie which had been saved for the "city hall" noncoms and the officers. He picked up a piece, bit into it, and scowled.

"Cold on top," he said.

"We should of took more time heating it," Mario said.

"We took more than enough time," Stan said, sampling. "It's burnt on the bottom."

Pyotr's spirits drooped. He had wanted the pie to be perfect. He thought of eating a piece himself to prove the others wrong, but then he heard a timid knock on the door.

Bellyrobber said, "Well, come on in, Tarzan."

The door opened, and in stepped a tall, slim rifleman. He was in his late teens, and Pyotr recognized him as the boy who had been sick at suppertime, back in the garden, many hours ago.

"I know I'm late," the young soldier said apologetically, "but I was way out there in a listening post—"

"And nobody relieved you 'til now?" Bellyrobber's granite

face softened. "Belly up to the table, son, and have yourself some pie."

The boy sat down but he didn't seem to know what to do with his rifle. Stan took the M-1, then lifted the heavy steel helmet from his head. Chuck put two pieces of pie into a mess kit, said, "Let city hall starve," and added a third piece to the pile. Mario brought a tin cup full of coffee, rich with canned milk. The boy smiled shyly at the cooks, but he didn't touch the pie.

Maybe his stomach is still upset, Pyotr thought worriedly.

"What's wrong?" Bellyrobber said. "Don't you like cherry pie?"

"I love cherry pie, sarge. Heck, I was raised on it. My mom baked the best—" He turned red in the lamplight. "I'm just tired, I guess."

Nervously he picked up a square of pie and bit into it. He sat there munching, frowning, and then his expression changed.

"Good?" Bellyrobber said.

The boy smiled happily.

"Sarge, this is the best doggone cherry pie I *ever* tasted!"

Pyotr gave the cookie tin he had been polishing one last hard rub, then held it up to the light. It was so shiny that he could see his face in the bottom. He bared his teeth and growled. The heat-warped metal mirrored a lopsided, lumpy-cheeked grin.

"*El hamdulillah!*" he said.

Chapter 10

BLACK DAY AT HORSESHOE GREEN

Pyotr awoke with a start. The rafters overhead told him that he was in the attic. He scanned the floor and saw several sleeping bags, all empty.

It must be late, he thought.

He unzipped his own sleeping bag and wriggled out. He pulled on and laced his old, thin-soled work shoes. He slapped his hat on his head, picked up his threadbare short coat and hurried down to the second floor.

Hearing half a dozen loud radio and telephone voices in the big front bedroom, he knew that this was no longer just the Oboe Company CP. Headquarters troops had moved in, and it was now Horseshoe Green, forward CP of the 4th Battalion, 112th Infantry.

On the ground floor he found S-2, the intelligence section, in the parlor for a change. Sergeant Nick Spiro was the Quiz Kid on duty. Nick cocked a devilish eyebrow at him.

"Sleep well, Russky?"

"I did indeed," Pyotr said. "Why was I not awakened?"

"I heard the kitchen crew talking about that," Nick said. "They agreed that you'd be safer asleep than awake—safer for them, that is."

"Hummm," Pyotr said. "Where did they go, sergeant?"

"To the rear to pick up that trailer-jeep you left in the middle of nowhere. After that they're going to load the kitchen truck and bring it forward."

"And where is Oboe Company now?"

"About three miles up ahead. They advanced fast for a while but now they're meeting stiff resistance."

Pyotr sighed. He had wanted so much to talk to Captain Croft last night, but an enemy patrol had touched off a lot of fireworks on Oboe's left flank, and the tall Texan had gone out to check his line. Before the captain returned, Bellyrobber had ordered Pyotr upstairs to bed—and here he was now, wondering what to do next.

He tipped back his hat and scratched his head.

"Stop that," Nick Spiro said.

"Stop what, sergeant?"

"Thinking, kiddo. I'm afraid you'll cook up something daffier than that cherry pie party last night—and trick me into helping you again."

He laughed at Pyotr's startled expression.

"Go eat breakfast, Russky, and stay out of mischief."

Pyotr's stomach agreed that this was a good idea. He went to the kitchen. He didn't know any of the Headquarters Company cooks, but they knew him.

"Bellyrobber said to stuff you good," the mess sergeant said, and when Pyotr left the kitchen his stomach bulged with pancakes, syrup, and bacon. He climbed the stairs and visited Message Center in the big bedroom. The joint, as the GIs themselves would say, was really jumping.

"Hi, Russky," said Sergeant Connors, the radio section chief. "Want to listen in?"

Pyotr nodded eagerly.

"We aren't using this SCR-300," Connors said. He tuned in the big field radio, then slid a headset over Pyotr's ears. "Be sure you root for the right side, Russky."

Magically, Pyotr entered another world. While shells and machine guns crumped and rattled in the background, he heard the battalion CO talking to one of his line company commanders.

"Green Three to Nan," Colonel MacCampbell was say-

ing. "Cossack Charlie reports he can't afford to send Big
Friend. You'll have to take that roadblock with organic
weapons." A bullet cracked in the air, and the colonel
added, "Over."

"Nan to Green Three," the N Company skipper's voice
said. "What organic weapons do you suggest, sir—sticks
and stones or B-B guns? Over."

"Green Three to Nan," the colonel said. "Don't give me
a hard time, Nan. You've heard of fire and movement. Use
it, man! Blind them with overhead fire, then rush . . ."

Pyotr stopped listening. The switchboard operator was
waving wildly at Lieutenant Snyder, the communications
officer. Snyder hurried toward the man, and Pyotr tore off
his headset to hear what they said.

"It's Oboe on the line, sir," the operator blurted. "A tree
burst just got Captain Croft!"

"Let me talk to the Oboe exec," Snyder snapped.

"He was hit by the same burst, sir. So was the first sergeant, and so was Bull Cotton. They're only wounded,
but . . ."

Pyotr dropped the headset. He walked quietly from the
room. The hands of the grandfather's clock at the end
of the hall pointed to 10:30. So early in the day, Pyotr
thought. A German shell burst high in the branches of a
tree, and the steel fragments came showering down, and in
a breath he was gone. KIA, the morning report will say.
Killed In Action. And that will be that, except for his family, and a few lonely GIs in foxholes who will always remember.

And Bull, he thought. How could *anything* hurt Bull?

But something had.

Suddenly he was running downstairs. Outside, he asked
the only jeep driver on duty to take him to Oboe Company.

"No," the man said. "I'm not taking any kid up into that
shellfire."

Pyotr thought of telling him that he had faced shellfire before—but there was another way.

"Where is the battalion aid station?" he asked.

"Up the main road about a quarter-mile, then up a side road about—hey, Russky, wait!"

Pyotr ran all the way.

The battalion aid station was in a well hidden farmhouse. Two stretcher-jeeps and an ambulance stood empty in the yard. Just as Pyotr reached the front door, it opened. He stepped aside to avoid being knocked down by a huge T-5 whose arms were so full of medical equipment that he couldn't see over the pile. The T-5 dumped his load into a jeep trailer and started for the door again. Then he noticed Pyotr.

"You're the kid they call Russky, aren't you?"

"That is correct, corporal."

"Well, I'm Bill Hill. They call me Big Bill."

"How do you do, Corporal Big Bill Hill?" Pyotr tried to smile as if he hadn't a worry in the world. "You seem to be preparing for a trip, corporal."

"Yeah. We're displacing forward."

"Ah, yes, the aid station should be closer to the line, corporal. I hear there are many casualties at Oboe Company."

Big Bill Hill nodded soberly. "Report just came in. Tree burst got a whole bunch of them."

"Will you, ah, will you be going to Oboe after you set up the new aid station, corporal?"

"Uh-uh. No need to. Line company aid men are supposed to see that the wounded get back to battalion. If they need extra stretcher bearers, they just borrow them from the company."

Pyotr thought fast. The medics might be willing to give him a ride to the new aid station, but also, they could refuse. He had better ask for GI clothing first. He freshened his smile.

"Corporal Hill," he said, "my feet are always cold and wet. Could you possibly spare an extra pair of shoepacs?"

"Why, sure, Russky. Come on in and I'll introduce you to the MAC."

Pyotr followed Big Bill inside. Several blanket-covered forms lay on stretchers in the parlor. Down the hall, two medics were easing another stretcher up out of the almost shellproof stone cavern of the cellar. Big Bill Hill led Pyotr into the dining room. The MAC, or medical administrative officer, turned out to be a short, stout captain who was packing surgical instruments into a metal chest.

"Captain Fritz, you've heard of Russky, haven't you?"

The MAC looked up. His eyes, like his face and his body, were quite round. But oddly, they did not match his black hair. They were baby-blue.

He said, "Hi, Russky. What's cooking?"

"Nothing in particular, sir. I just dropped in—"

"He needs a pair of shoepacs, captain," Big Bill said.

The round, baby-blue eyes wandered innocently over Pyotr, from head to foot and back again.

"He needs a whole new outfit, corporal. Why don't you take him out back and fix him up?"

"Out back" proved to be a small storeroom next to the kitchen. Pyotr looked inside and gloated.

"Just pick out what you want and put it on," Big Bill said. "I'll be with you after we finish loading the vehicles."

Big Bill's loading chore took some time. When he finally did return to the storeroom he took one look at Pyotr and said, "Wow! Wait 'til the MAC sees this!"

In the dining room, Captain Fritz was fully dressed for a cold jeep ride. At sight of Pyotr he yanked off his helmet and slammed it down on the table.

"Well," he said, "you certainly believe in doing things up brown, don't you, Russky?"

"Brown, sir?"

"Thorough. But never mind. Are you wearing GI underwear?"

"No, sir. It doesn't seem quite sanitary to wear someone else's underwear."

"You have a good point there, Russky. But you *are* wearing GI shoepacs, trousers, shirt, field jacket, gloves, pistol belt, canteen—and although I can't see them, probably a GI sweater, wool cap, and first aid kit." Captain Fritz closed one round blue eye and opened the other wider. "Not to mention a GI steel helmet, ammo pouches, and carbine. What do you expect to do with the carbine, my ambitious young friend?"

Pyotr could not stand the MAC's one-eyed stare. He looked down at the helmet on the table. Being a Medical Corps helmet, it featured a large red cross in the middle of a larger white disc. Even the red-and-white bull's-eye stared him down. He studied a floral pattern on the carpet.

"Hand me that GI overcoat you've got so carefully folded over your arm, Russky."

Pyotr obeyed. Without looking up, he knew that the MAC was examining the sleeves.

"You tore off the chevrons, Russky. Do you have them in your pocket?"

Pyotr surrendered the chevrons silently. All he had wanted to do was pose as a real combat soldier, so he could hitch a ride out on the main road. The buck sergeant's stripes would have helped, even if he was a bit young for that rank. But what was the use? This little fat man . . .

"I received two calls from the CP before you arrived," the MAC said. "They were quite concerned about a young Russian boy who had run off alone, heading our way. Now understand me, Russky. You are *not* a soldier. You are an underage civilian. I want that helmet, and that carbine. And take those ammunition pouches off your belt—"

Captain Fritz's voice stopped abruptly. Pyotr looked up, puzzled. The MAC was grinning at him!

"But keep everything else, Russky. You'll need warm clothes for a cold jeep ride."

"You mean—you're taking me forward, sir?"

"Why not? The new aid station is pretty well concealed in a draw, so there shouldn't be too much danger. And besides, Bull Cotton is your buddy as well as mine. I think you've got a right to say good-by before they cart him off to the hospital."

Pyotr sat down limply in the nearest chair.

"This is no time for combat exhaustion," the MAC said. "Let's field-test that baggy uniform of yours out on the road."

In the yard again, Pyotr saw that the ambulance and one stretcher-jeep had gone, bearing their loads of wounded to the rear. Big Bill Hill sat at the wheel of the remaining jeep, breathing jets of steam into the icy air.

"Main road or side road, sir?" he asked as Captain Fritz and Pyotr climbed into the back seat.

"Side road, corporal. It's a longer route, but safer."

Big Bill swung the jeep into the rutted, lane-like side road. Pyotr turned to Captain Fritz.

"Sir, you said Sergeant Cotton was a buddy of yours. Are you a veteran of the Bulge too?"

MAC Fritz laughed.

"Bulge, Hürtgen, hedgerows—you name the campaign and I'm a veteran. Fact is, I'm one of the Original Pennsylvanians, Russky. I've rolled with the 28th ever since Indiantown Gap."

Pyotr knew the story of the Bloody Bucket very well by now. The division had been federalized in 1940, and had assembled at Indiantown Gap, Pennsylvania. Many of the

National Guardsmen had been transferred to other units before the 28th shipped overseas, but many, many more filled hospitals and graves from the Channel to the Rhine. MAC Fritz was one of a gallant handful of survivors.

"So you've been with the outfit even longer than Sergeant Cotton," Pyotr said with respect.

"Oh, yes. Bull didn't join up 'til Florida maneuvers. I first saw him the day he carried Tim Gannon into the dispensary. Tim had been bitten by a cottonmouth moccasin—"

"A what, sir?"

"A poisonous snake, Russky. Its bite is often fatal. In Tim's case it wasn't because Bull had sucked out a lot of blood and applied a tourniquet. I gave Tim an antisnake shot and he was okay again in a few days."

Pyotr nodded thoughtfully.

"This Tim Gannon, sir. Are you referring to Lieutenant Gannon, the intelligence officer?"

"Of course. His first name is Timothy."

Pyotr shook his head in mild wonder. "Imagine," he said, "Greasegun Gannon bitten by a snake!"

"Tim was only a rookie then," MAC Fritz said, chuckling. "He didn't earn his nickname until we hit combat."

"Was Bull a rookie too, sir?"

"That's right. They were both fresh out of basic training."

Hundreds of yards away, enemy shells cr-r-rumped on the main road. Pyotr ignored them.

"Sir," he said, "I don't understand the Army."

"Don't try," MAC Fritz said. "Just stick with the outfit and hope to stay sane."

"Yes, sir. But it may help if you can tell me why Private Gannon became an officer and Private Cotton didn't."

The MAC seemed to hesitate. Then he said, "Well, Tim had an edge in education, Russky."

"But not in intelligence, sir. And as for leadership qualities it is hard to choose between them. The men in Oboe say the colonel never assigned an officer to the third platoon because Bull was the best platoon leader in the battalion, regardless of rank. Is that true, sir?"

"Yes," MAC Fritz said slowly, "it's true. But—"

He grunted as Big Bill Hill swerved into the ditch. Around the bend came a jeep and tarpaulin-covered trailer. Three pairs of booted feet extended beyond the back rim of the trailer. The pairs of combat boots jumped up and down, up and down, performing a jerky, out-of-step jig because the legs of the men under the tarpaulin were stiff with rigor mortis.

"Graves Registration jeep," Big Bill said. "Those meat wagons give me the creeps."

Captain Fritz did not reply, and Pyotr could not. Rank had ceased to be important. Was Bull Cotton still alive, or was he riding to his grave in that trailer?

CHAPTER 11

SITTING BULL'S LAST STAND

The new aid station was a long, narrow, slate-roofed stone shed, nestled deep in a wooded draw. Piles of staves littered the shed's loading platform, and Pyotr guessed it was a storage house for kegs of ripening wine.

He dreaded what he might learn when he stepped inside.

Big Bill and MAC Fritz jumped out of the jeep. They hurried into the shed. Pyotr dragged his feet to the edge of the loading platform and stopped. The lone soldier sitting so forlornly on that pile of barrel staves looked familiar. He had taken off his helmet but not his wool knit cap, and the snug cap made his small head seem positively tiny. Pyotr smiled, remembering. This stooped, dead-beat GI belonged to Bull Cotton's own third platoon. He walked toward the man.

"Hello," he said, "Private Peahead Willoughby."

The small head turned.

"Hi, Russky-boy. How you doin'?"

"Fine, thank you. How are you, Peahead?"

"Better than some." Peahead opened the overcoat which was draped over his shoulders, and showed a bandaged arm in a sling. "Leastways I'm walkin' wounded."

"Oh," Pyotr said. "I thought you were a member of the Oboe carrying party."

"Nope. They went back to the company ten minutes ago." Peahead licked his chapped, cracked lips. "How come you're so far forward today, Russky?"

"I came to visit Bull Cotton," Pyotr said.

"I thought so." Peahead clucked sadly. "Poor ole Bull. He's got a hole in his shoulder you could poke a thumb through, but he wouldn't come with us."

"You mean he stayed at Oboe? Why, Peahead?"

"Because they ain't but two officers left, neither of 'em with much combat experience. Bull swears he's goin' to hang on 'til Green Three sends him a CO with enough savvy to take charge."

Pyotr groaned.

"Good luck, Peahead," he said, and ran toward the end of the draw.

He stayed on the side road until it dipped into the valley, then struck out across the fields, heading for the main road that offered a shorter route to Oboe Company. In one battle-torn strip of field he came upon a former German strongpoint, three machine-gun pits linked by slit trenches. Near the last pit he found a GI helmet with a long gash along the side, and a carbine in perfect condition. He slung the carbine on his shoulder, put on the helmet, and ran faster, loose helmet bouncing, loose overcoat flapping around his legs with every stride.

Five minutes later he clambered over a stone fence, vaulted a ditch, and landed on the main road. There he paused for repairs. First he tightened the headband of the helmet until it hugged his head. Then he threw away the tent-sized overcoat, shortened his pistol belt, and buckled it over his field jacket. Finally he picked up the carbine again and dogtrotted up the road—looking, he hoped, like a small but tough runner with a battle-scarred helmet on his way to deliver an important message.

Behind him, a jeep motor growled. He turned and waved, but the driver didn't even slow down. As the stubby vehicle zoomed past, he noticed the vertical white line on the back of the passenger's helmet. An officer, he thought. Well, Oboe needs officers in a hurry.

Half a mile farther on, he passed a wire crew checking a snakelike tangle of wires in the ditch. At the end of a full mile a hidden sentry halted him.

"Golden," the sentry said.

"Gate," Pyotr gasped. "Where is the CP?"

"Under that cliff," the sentry said. "You'll have to look sharp to find it, soldier."

Soldier!

"What is it like?" Pyotr asked.

"It's a sort of dugout-tent. The boys had to work fast but it looks like a bump in the cliff."

Pyotr ran on, realizing only now that Oboe Company must have slowed to a halt or there wouldn't even be a CP. Scouting the cliff, he found the "bump." With no house handy this time, the GIs had simply laid a few poles across a natural notch in the cliff, then hung clay-smeared tarpaulins over the poles. The result was a marvel of camouflage.

He raised the entrance tarp and stood up inside the CP.

"You little devil," a strange, hoarse voice said. "What are you doing here?"

A lantern hung directly in front of Pyotr. He sidestepped, squinting through the glare.

Bull Cotton was sitting on an ammunition box, leaning back against the clay wall. Except for the field jacket thrown over his shoulders, he was bare to the waist. His right arm rested in a sling and a thick wad of taped bandages covered his right shoulder and half of his chest. The bandages were soggy with blood.

Pyotr's eyes flicked from right to left. Hank Santos, a company aid man, was straddling a K-ration box. Ralph Knudsen, runner, was sitting on his folded poncho. The fourth man in the dark, dank dugout was a second lieutenant. He leaned forward on his ammo box, and lantern light glinted on his new gold bars. In spite of his strapping size, he was the youngest looking American officer Pyotr had ever seen.

Then the lieutenant spoke.

"Sergeant Cotton, I demand—"

"At ease, junior," Bull said. "Russky, I asked you what you're doing here."

"I heard you were wounded, sergeant. I came—"

Bull Cotton grinned, gasped, and gritted his teeth. Pyotr could almost feel the pain himself.

"Sure was nice of you to come," Bull said, breathing hard.

"Isn't there something I can do, sergeant?"

"No, Russky, thank you kindly. All I need is a new company commander that's big enough for the job—and if it isn't asking Santa Claus for too much, a couple of platoon leaders that are fit to lead platoons."

Pyotr glanced at the young lieutenant. The boy was trying very hard to hold back his anger.

"Sergeant Cotton," he said, "let's be reasonable. If you'll just pick up the phone and call battalion—"

"The wire is cut," Bull said. "Shellfire somewhere. As for radio, we lost contact more than an hour ago when we were advancing fast. The hills are too high for the batteries. So I'm telling you one more time—"

"But as I told *you* before, I'm a qualified platoon leader. You admit there are only two officers in the outfit. If one of them acts as CO, that leaves only one officer at platoon level. Think of it, sergeant—a rifle company in heavy combat with three leaderless platoons!"

"Leaderless!" Bull Cotton bellowed, and now he sounded like his old self. "There are three good platoon sergeants out there. Better men than you'll ever be if you live to a hundred—"

The lieutenant leaped to his feet.

"I've stood this insubordinate nonsense long enough!" he

shouted. "You say you're the acting executive officer until the new CO arrives. I say you're a raving madman. I'm going out there and take over—"

Bull Cotton brought his left arm out of the shadows behind his ammo box. Suddenly his big fist was full of gun— Captain Croft's pearl-handled six-gun!

"What!" the lieutenant gasped. "You're threatening a commissioned officer with a gun?"

Bull rested his Colt-heavy hand on his knee.

"It ain't a bean-shooter," he said.

Out on the road, a motor purred. Every head in the dugout turned toward the sound.

"Now we shall see what we shall see," the lieutenant said, and sat down on his ammo box.

Feet slopped mushily in clay and snow. Plump fingers raised the entrance tarp. A red-and-white bull's-eye helmet appeared, followed by a short, round body.

MAC Fritz smiled apologetically.

"Bull," he said, "I have orders to bring you back alive."

"Who gave the orders, doc?"

"Douglas A. MacCampbell, lieutenant colonel, USA. Horseshoe Green Three himself."

"Green Three owes me one company commander in good working order," Bull said. "When he produces, I'll go back with you. But not one minute before, doc."

MAC Fritz looked Bull over carefully. "Hummm," he said, and sat down on a vacant ammo box.

"How's the patient doing?" he asked Santos, the aid man.

"Hurting bad," Santos said, "and getting weaker in spite of the bluff he's putting up. The splinter that hit him is still in there, sawing at his collarbone every time he moves. I taped on two pressure bandages and about a mile of gauze but he keeps right on bleeding."

"Do you have more dressings in your bag?"

"Yes, sir."

"Good. I'll change his bandages myself."

MAC Fritz stood up. Bull Cotton's cold stare rose with him.

"Stay put, doc. I don't trust you."

"Why Bull! How can you say a thing like that?"

"Cut the comedy, doc. You used to be a lean-bellied wrestler at Penn State. You'd like nothing better than to clamp some kind of fancy hold on me and drag me out to that stretcher-jeep. Well, don't try it, or you'll take a ride in your own stretcher."

MAC Fritz sighed. He sat down for the second time—and the young lieutenant exploded.

"Sir," he said in a strangled voice, "how can you let an enlisted man talk to you like that?"

"I am a poor, unarmed, helpless pillroller," MAC Fritz said. "How can I stop him?"

"You can—you can—"

"By the way, lieutenant, we haven't been introduced. My name is Luther Fritz. What's yours?"

"Van Alstyne, sir. Pomeroy Van Alstyne. But—"

"Delighted to meet you." MAC Fritz practically forced the furious young man to shake his hand. "Just graduated from Officer Candidate School, eh, Van?"

Pomeroy Van Alstyne couldn't hold back a proud smile.

"I pinned these gold bars on just a month ago," he said, "and here I am!" He wiped off the smile. "Now, sir, why can't you order this stupid noncom—"

"He isn't really stupid," MAC Fritz said. "Believe it or not, he has an IQ over 130. He could have gone to OCS too, Van."

Pomeroy Van Alstyne sat there, trying to digest this large, lumpy, indigestible fact.

"You're wondering why he didn't go?" MAC Fritz asked.

Pomeroy Van Alstyne nodded wordlessly.

"Because he lacked the guts," MAC Fritz said.

"Now wait a minute, doc!"

Bull's voice was so hoarse now that it sounded like the bullfrog croak of Haj Ali El Fassy. Pyotr threw a quick glance at him. Bull's back had slid down the wall. He was slumping on his ammo box, trying to hold his head up.

"You disagree, Bull?" the MAC inquired politely.

"Yeah. You ain't being fair. My folks were dirt poor. I couldn't go to college—"

"You didn't need college for OCS. All you needed was high school, intelligence, and enough gumption to prove your leadership ability at a higher level."

"M-m-my grammar was lousy," Bill muttered. "Enlisted men don't respect an officer that sounds ignorant, even if he—even if he—ain't."

"Quit saying 'ain't' on purpose," MAC Fritz snapped. "You could straighten out your grammar in a week."

"But—" Bull grimaced, blinking, as if puzzled. "Say, doc, haven't we been through all this before?" He raised his gun hand and wiped his forearm across his eyes. "Sure we have. I remember—"

"So do I," MAC Fritz said. "Twice I tried to persuade you to face the challenge of your lifetime, and twice you chickened out." He shook his head and gave a grunt of contempt. "Well, look at yourself now, Bull—a man born to lead other men in a crisis, forced to pull a gun on a half-baked shavetail because he outranks you!"

An awful silence filled the room. Bull Cotton's chin sank down to his chest, and his gun hand was shaking uncontrollably. Pomeroy Van Alstyne glared at the little fat man who had called him a half-baked shavetail, but MAC Fritz had eyes only for Bull. Pyotr watched them all, in turn, and at last MAC Fritz broke the silence.

"You think you own Oboe Company," he said, "but you don't even own the gun you're holding. You're just a power-less noncom trying to pull a bluff on an officer, and you're not fooling anybody." He paused again, sneering brutally. "You're through, Bull. You're through, and you're pathetic."

All of a sudden Pomeroy Van Alstyne stood up, tall and young and strong.

"He's pathetic, all right," he said, "and I intend to take that gun away from him."

He took a step toward Bull. Bull's left hand came up, but the six-gun wobbled. Pomeroy Van Alstyne took another step, and Pyotr unslung his carbine.

Out on the road, a jeep motor snarled, then cut off abruptly. Big Bill Hill, Pyotr thought absently, or the lieutenant's driver, gunning his motor to make sure it will start again in the cold.

Pomeroy Van Alstyne took a third step toward Bull. Pyotr reversed his carbine, holding the butt forward. And then Bull Cotton mumbled "Pathetic, huh?" and toppled to the floor.

"Ahhh!" said Pomeroy Van Alstyne. He reached for the big pearl-handled six-shooter.

Pyotr threw the carbine butt first, like a spear. It hit the hinge of Pomeroy Van Alstyne's jaw with a sodden thump. For a split second, Pomeroy Van Alstyne seemed to hang in the air, hand outstretched, ready to pick up the gun. Then he made a sound like a punctured tire, rammed his already damaged jaw into the soft clay of the floor, and collapsed beside Bull Cotton.

"Russky, Russky," MAC Fritz said sadly. "Why did you have to spoil it? I was all set to clamp a hammerlock on him."

"I don't care what you were going to do," Pyotr shouted, shrill with fear for himself, fear for Bull, and anger for anybody else. "How could you say such terrible things about Bull?"

"I was just stalling," MAC Fritz said. "I wanted to tire

him out, make him faint quickly. Insulting him was the easiest way, so—"

He turned around, facing the entrance tarp. Pyotr heard boots squishing in clay. He saw a big, freckled hand raise the tarp, and there stood Greasegun Gannon.

Greasegun took in the scene and whistled.

"What is this," he said, "a wake?"

Nobody answered.

"Don't tell me they knocked each other out," he said.

Still nobody answered.

Greasegun Gannon pitched his helmet into a corner, eased the stubby submachine gun off his shoulder, and sat down on Pomeroy Van Alstyne's unoccupied ammo box.

"Okay," he said, "I'll get the facts when they come to. Meanwhile, Fritzie, Green Three is hopping mad. He says you're to get Bull to the aid station without delay. He also said, and I quote, 'When Bull Cotton gets out of the hospital, he's going to accept a battlefield commission if I have to stuff it down his stubborn throat.' End quote." Greasegun squinted at Bull, who was beginning to stir. "How is he, doc?"

"He'll make it, Tim, but he needs a blood transfusion fast." MAC Fritz jabbed a finger at Santos. "Get him out to that jeep on the double."

At that moment, Pomeroy Van Alstyne groaned. He rolled over on his side, raised himself on one elbow and searched the dugout with glazed eyes. He saw no guilt in any face except that of the young foreign boy, who couldn't possibly hurt a fly, so he rubbed his sore jaw and sat up.

"Who did it?" he said. "I demand—"

Greasegun Gannon threw back his head and filled the dugout with gales of laughter. He wore no insignia of rank, and to all appearances he was just a big, burly, redheaded, freckle-faced private sitting on an ammo box and having a very good time at a very bad time.

"At ease, soldier!" Pomeroy Van Alstyne barked. "Who are you and what are you doing here?"

Greasegun Gannon stopped laughing.

"I'm the new skipper of Oboe Company," he said, "and I'm here to take command."

"Oh," Pomeroy Van Alstyne said.

"You mean 'Oh, sir,'" Greasegun said. "But I'll attend to you in a minute."

Santos and Knudsen had lifted Bull onto a rifle-and-blanket stretcher. Now they carried him to Greasegun. Bull put out his left hand and Greasegun took it.

"So long, Tim," Bull said, "and don't feel bad about losing that Intelligence job. You'll be better off up here where you don't need brains, old buddy."

"Thanks, old buddy," Greasegun said. "Get well quick and hurry back. The one thing we need most in this outfit is an executive officer who can't read or write."

They grinned at each other, hands locked tight. Then the stretcher bearers carried Bull outside, and Greasegun Gannon turned to Pomeroy Van Alstyne.

"You!" he said. "Get those sniper-baiting gold bars off your shoulders. Then report to Tubby Schmidt, the third platoon sergeant. Yes, I said *report*. In a few minutes I'm going to start this company rolling again and it's going to get awfully hairy out there. You need somebody to teach you how to stay alive in combat and Tubby is a good teacher. If you're a good pupil, if you keep your trap shut and learn fast, you may live. But if you want it the other way—"

MAC Fritz touched Pyotr's elbow.

"Let's get out of here," he whispered, "before Pomeroy Van Alstyne talks back."

Pyotr followed him outside.

"Well, Russky," he said, "Bull's dream finally came true. What do you think of that?"

"I think it's wonderful," Pyotr said, "if becoming an officer really was his dream."

"Sure it was. You see, Bull grew up in a poverty-stricken
mining town in Kentucky. He sees himself as crude, unedu-
cated—unfit to be an officer. But that was his dream, just
the same." MAC Fritz chuckled. "When I was a kid I
thrived on dreams and buckwheat cakes. One day I dis-
covered an anatomy book, and after that I dreamed of being a doctor." He patted his stomach. "So that's what I am
today—a Pennsylvania Dutch chowhound-M.D."

Pyotr laughed, and MAC Fritz eyed him shrewdly.

"Every boy has a dream, Russky. What's yours?"

"I dream of going to America and studying languages,"
Pyotr said. "I love the magic of words. I love the sound of
speech. Sir, do you realize how many different accents
Americans have?"

"Dozens, I suppose."

"Thousands!" Pyotr said. "I could study speech forever!"

MAC Fritz put an arm around his shoulder.

"Be patient," he said. "This war can't last forever—"

Far behind them, Greasegun Gannon's voice rose to a
roar. It reminded Pyotr of a hungry tiger being fed in the
Kiev zoo.

"Poor Pomeroy Van Alstyne," he said. "He must have
talked back."

Chapter 12

STICK WITH THE OUTFIT

Simone, captain of waitresses at the inter-Allied mess, wore a uniform of her own invention: French Army beret, British Army battle jacket, U. S. Army trousers, and female civilian wedgies. Her kewpie doll smile charmed every Allied male who entered the big international mess, and Pyotr was no exception.

"*Bonjour*, Russky," she said. "You are fashionably late for breakfast, *mon petit chou*."

"I'm sorry, Mademoiselle Simone. French feather beds will spoil me yet."

"*Bon!*" she said. "But a gentleman has been waiting to see you. An officer. Follow me, *s'il vous plaît*."

Her doll-like legs carried her at a great rate past long rows of enlisted men's bench-tables. She invaded the officers' section and stopped at a chair-table.

"Sir," she said, "this is the young man you wished to see. Captain Wilson—Monsieur Russky!"

Captain Wilson was a tall, thin, bony officer with a bristly GI haircut, steel-rimmed GI glasses, long jaw, and hollow cheeks. At first glance he looked like an undertaker in uniform, but when he smiled his gaunt face glowed.

"Glad to meet you, Russky. Please sit down."

Simone pulled out a chair, shoved it under Pyotr's legs, and sat him down with a bang.

"Pancakes or eggs?" she asked.

"Well," Pyotr said, "let me see—"

"Both," she said, and vanished.

Pyotr turned to find Captain Wilson studying him. He felt uneasy. He started to ask what this meeting was about, but the officer spoke first.

"I visited Horseshoe Green last weekend, Russky. They seem to think a lot of you over there."

Pyotr blushed, tried to smile, and blushed harder.

"No shells this morning, sir," he said hurriedly to cover his confusion. "A whole week without shells. It seems like a miracle—and thank God it's true."

"Do you thank God often, Russky?"

"I—I—well, yes, sir, I do. It's a habit infantrymen fall into, you know, if they stay alive."

Captain Wilson's gray eyes glinted with amusement. Pyotr began to like him.

"By the way," the captain said, "I saw that parade the 4th Battalion put on last Saturday. I wasn't nearly as impressed when the whole Bloody Bucket rolled down the Champs-Elysées." He tapped his heart. "It hit me right here, Russky."

Pyotr knew what he meant. He had heard much about the 28th Division's grand march down the Champs-Elysées to celebrate the liberation of Paris. It must have been splendid. But he had *seen* the little parade near Walbach, and he would never forget it as long as he lived.

The guns were silent. The only Germans left in the Colmar Pocket were prisoners. Once again all Alsace belonged to France, and the French were grateful for American help in winning back the lost province. They had sent the band of the famous Foreign Legion to Walbach, and the villagers had gone wild with joy at sight of the gallant desert fighters. Pyotr admired the Foreign Legionnaires, but they were not his heroes. Let the French blow the horns and beat the drums, he had thought that day. I have eyes only for those red keystones shining down the line. There goes *my* outfit!

The GIs had passed in review over a rocky, sloping hill-side meadow. Wounds and death had taken their toll, but to Pyotr, standing on the sidelines, those under-strength rifle companies had seemed mighty beyond compare.

He could see Oboe Company now, with Greasegun Gannon out in front, proudly wearing that pearl-handled six-gun. And Tubby Schmidt, and Hank Santos, and Ralph Knudsen, and Bellyrobber Bass, and Mario Poggi, and Stan Polski, and Chuck Jenkins, and even Pomeroy Van Alstyne, looking strangely older now. Yes, he could see them, all of them, the men who marched in the flesh, and the men who marched only in spirit—Bud Parente, Captain Tex Croft, and all the others who had given their lives—and he knew in his heart that finer soldiers had yet to be born. . . .

A big metal tray appeared before him.

"Pancakes and eggs and sausages and syrup and canned strawberries and milk," Simone said "*Bon appétit, mon petit soldat!*"

She trotted away, leaving Pyotr to wonder how he could eat all that food. Across the table, Captain Wilson was thumbing tobacco into a briar pipe.

"It was a great parade, sir," he said. "I think I have never seen a more inspiring sight than the Stars and Stripes rippling in the breeze. And the regimental colors—all those battle streamers! I hadn't realized the old 112th had been in so many battles."

"A lot of battles in several wars," Captain Wilson said. He frowned thoughtfully. "Of course courage knows no nationality. You've seen American, German, and Russian troops, Russky. Which are the best, really?"

"The Americans, sir."

"Why?"

"Because they are free," Pyotr said. "I don't mean they lack discipline. It's just that"—he couldn't find the right words, so he waved his fork—"that they've been brought up to think for themselves. So when a crisis occurs—when a leader is killed, for instance—a new leader is always there to meet the emergency."

"You've seen this happen?"

"Yes, sir, right in Oboe Company. And you saw the results in that victory parade last Saturday."

"Fair enough, as a military example," Captain Wilson said. "But what about a crisis in American civilian life? Would the new leader appear just as naturally?"

"Why not?" Pyotr said. "Tex Croft and Greasegun Gannon were both products of American civilian life. It must be good."

For a moment Captain Wilson's bony face glowed. Then the glow snapped off like a light.

"They were products of democracy," he said. "I take it that you approve of democracy?"

Pyotr speared a three-layer piece of pancake, then added a half-link of sausage. He stirred his loaded fork in a puddle of syrup but did not raise the fork to his mouth. He was not nearly as hungry as he had thought a few minutes ago. He looked up and met the captain's gray eyes.

"From what I have seen," he said, "democracy is wonderful. But if I am to learn more about it, I must first find a way to get to America."

Captain Wilson's pipe had gone out. He produced another match and puffed busily.

"I hear there's a man from UNRRA, the new refugee organization, here in Colmar," he said. "Did you come to Colmar to see him?"

Pyotr nodded. "Lieutenant Gannon thought UNRRA would be a good source of information about naturalization. My friend Pfc Lindner drove me here, but the UNRRA man hadn't arrived. Pfc Lindner had to return to the Fourth Battalion, so he secured lodgings for me and gave me a ticket to the inter-allied mess. Mademoiselle Simone has been most kind—but if the UNRRA man doesn't come to-day I don't know what I shall do. There are rumors that the 28th has orders to roll again. It could happen at any time—"

Now his appetite was all gone. He laid down his fork and pushed the tray away from him.

"I must not be left behind," he said, "yet I must find out whether or not I have anything to hope for."

Captain Wilson puffed on the briar pipe, frowning, gray eyes slitted, staring across the wide expanse of the mess hall. Suddenly Pyotr noticed something peculiar about his uniform. He wore the twin silver "railroad tracks" of his rank on his field jacket, but the collar tabs of his OD shirt were bare. There were no ornaments, such as rifles, cannon, or castles, to indicate his arm or service. What did the man *do* in the Army . . . ?

"Russky," the captain said, "I hear you're from Kiev, in the Ukraine."

"That is correct, sir."

"The Ukranians have a long history of resistance to Russia, and to Communism, too. Did your parents share the typical Ukranian dislike of the Soviet Union?"

I should have known, Pyotr thought. He's a G-2 officer, assigned to investigate me.

"My parents were not Ukranians," he said levelly. "They were Russians, Great Russians who moved to Kiev before I was born. My mother died when I was a small child. My father was anti-Communist, but living in the Ukraine had nothing to do with it. He was a moral man, a man of principle. He was a loyal Russian. He hated Communism because he thought it was essentially evil."

There was a long silence.

"I see," Captain Wilson said finally. "And your brothers?"

"They were not political," Pyotr said. "They died defending their country from the Nazis, that is all."

Captain Wilson seemed to nod without moving his head. The gray eyes probed mercilessly.

"But your sister, Russky—she was a Communist, wasn't she?"

Pyotr drew in a deep breath.

"My sister married a Communist Party official," he said. "I grieve for her as if she were dead." He stood up. "Please excuse me, captain. I must go now."

"Wait a minute," the captain said, and stood up also. "I think it would be a good idea if we saw this UNRRA man together. Do you mind?"

"Not at all, sir," Pyotr said drearily.

They walked to the entrance. They picked up their helmets and overcoats and put them on.

"*Au revoir*, Russky," Simone said. "Good luck today."

"Thank you, Mademoiselle Simone," he said. "And if I do not see you again—God bless you."

She blew him a kiss, and he walked out.

"The UNRRA office is just around the corner," the captain said, "but for reasons I'll explain later, we must hurry."

Pyotr didn't answer. The captain laid a bony hand on his shoulder and almost pushed him along. He hated the hand but was afraid to brush it off.

When he saw the long line of shabby civilians waiting in the street he knew that the UNRRA man was there. Captain Wilson led him straight through the front door and into a big room where more shabby civilians sat waiting on benches. A young woman in a plain brown uniform came forward, smiling.

"This is an emergency, miss," the captain said. "I must see the person in charge immediately."

"Why certainly, captain. Just wait by the office door."

Five minutes dragged by. Pyotr looked at the ceiling, the floor, Captain Wilson's collar tabs—everywhere but at the miserable, fear-ridden people who filled the room. Then the door opened, the girl in the UNRRA uniform said, "You may go in now, captain," and Pyotr followed Captain Wilson into the office.

A big bald-headed man was sitting at a small battered desk.

"Good morning," he said in heavily accented English. "My name is Ionescu. Sit down and tell me about it."

Captain Wilson sat down. So did Pyotr.

"My young friend here," the captain said, "is a refugee, informally employed by the 28th Division, United States Army. He wants to become an American citizen. What can be done about it, Mr. Ionescu?"

Mr. Ionescu rocked back in his swivel chair, whistled at the ceiling, and leaned forward again.

"Captain," he said, "millions of Europeans are homeless. Hundreds of thousands are stateless. And they all want to become American citizens. Are you sure you don't just want to find a place for him in a camp for displaced persons?"

"Quite sure." Captain Wilson's voice was so crisp it seemed to crackle. "I want him to be a citizen."

Pyotr sat very still. He watched Mr. Ionescu rub his eyelids as if he were very tired.

"What is the boy's nationality, captain?"

"Russian."

Mr. Ionescu winced. Then he gestured toward a book which lay open on his cluttered desk.

"I could go through the motions of checking the figures for you," he said, "but I know them by heart. The immigration quota for the Soviet Union is exactly 2712 souls per year—and last year, 1944, exactly forty-one Russians became naturalized American citizens."

"Why only forty-one, Mr. Ionescu?"

"The United States and the Soviet Union are wartime allies now, captain, but for twenty years they quarantined each other. The Soviets didn't want their people to leave

Russia, and American officials were equally anxious to keep possible Communist subversives out of the U.S.A. This two-way boycott has eased since 1941, but in its place we now have a human log jam of DPs who all want to be American citizens. Also, *any* candidate for citizenship from *any* country must prove that he can support himself while he is living in the States and waiting for his final papers. He needs sponsors, responsible U.S. citizens who can guarantee that he will not become a public charge." Mr. Ionescu paused. "Tell me, captain, is there anyone *now in the United States* who can accept responsibility for the support of this school-age youth from the Soviet Union?"

Captain Wilson shook his head slowly.

"The only Americans who even know he exists are GIs," he said. "Right now they're fighting over here. Later, of course, when they go back home—"

"That may be late indeed," Mr. Ionescu said. "Quite likely they will have to serve in Germany as occupation troops." He reached up and thoughtfully massaged his pink scalp. "Still, there may be a possibility in that very fact. How old is the boy, captain?"

"Fifteen, sir," Pyotr answered for himself. "I shall be sixteen in two more months."

"So you speak English! What is your name?"

"Pyotr Dmitrievich Pribylov, sir."

"What languages do you speak, besides Russian and English?"

"German, Polish, a little French, a smattering of—"

Mr. Ionescu held up his hand.

"Pyotr," he said, "why don't you just go on working for the Army for two more years? Then, when you are eighteen, you can enlist—if you still want to."

"If I still want to? I don't understand, sir."

"After the war we'll have a big occupation force in Germany. The military will employ thousands of civilians, and

I'm sure qualified European volunteers will be permitted to enlist in the Army. So with good connections and a good command of languages you'll be able to make a living as either a soldier or civilian." Mr. Ionescu smiled slyly. "Of course, naturalization is quick and easy in the service. Thousands of foreign-born GIs have become citizens in less than half the time it took a foreign civilian like me to make it."

"You mean," Pyotr said, "all I have to do is stick with the outfit?"

"Not quite all, but—" Mr. Ionescu nodded toward the door. "Many of those poor people out there will be homeless for years. Oh, we'll provide food and clothing and shelter for them, but a camp is not a home, and waiting in idleness can be sheer agony." He sighed, then brightened. "Like them, you must wait, but you will be free, doing useful work. Beyond that, I only know that your future home is at least in sight. You have something to hope for, something to strive for."

"That is all I ask," Pyotr said.

One minute later, Pyotr and Captain Wilson stepped out into the waiting room. Halfway down the aisle, the girl in the UNRRA uniform was trying to pacify a tall, burly, red-faced, loud-voiced American major.

"Joe!" the major shouted. "What have you been up to?"

"Following your instructions," Captain Wilson said calmly. "I mousetrapped him in the inter-allied mess, questioned him thoroughly, and then brought him here."

"You call that following instructions? Sure, I asked you to pick him up at the mess—but then you were supposed to take him to Division so I could question him!" The major swore explosively. "I waited and waited, Joe! When you didn't show up I went over to the mess. Simone said you'd probably taken him to UNRRA, so I came here. All that time wasted—"

"Now, Pete," Captain Wilson said, "no time was wasted.

"What I found out about this boy would satisfy any reasonable man. Won't you take my word for it?"

Major Pete glanced sharply at Pyotr, then turned back to Captain Wilson.

"Well, I certainly can't interrogate him now," he grumbled. "The whole division is set to roll." He sledged the air with a *Panzerfaust*-sized fist. "But Joe, there isn't any place for an unscreened foreigner in a troop movement like this!"

"I'll vouch for him," Captain Wilson said. "In fact, I'll take him with me. We'll stop at Horseshoe Green just long enough to clear it with his CO, and then we'll ride together the rest of the way. I'll keep an eye on him constantly, Pete. I promise."

Major Pete snorted, then gave a grudging nod.

"Okay, Joe, have it your way. We'll take it up again when we get there." He checked his watch. "I've got to get back to the CP. Have a good trip, but"—he glanced at Pyotr again—"oh, never mind!"

He strode to the front door, whipped it open, and slammed it behind him. Pyotr and Captain Wilson followed, much more slowly.

"Sir," Pyotr said, "who was that officer?"

"Major Pete Prescott, Division G-2. An intelligence officer." Captain Wilson closed his bony hand on Pyotr's shoulder and squeezed gently. "Your Greasegun Gannon was a little concerned about you, Russky. He wanted to be sure you got through with UNRRA and back to Oboe Company in time for the big move, so he phoned Division hoping to find somebody who might be willing to help you. At that point everything went wrong. The first officer he spoke to got suspicious and switched the call to G-2—"

"And Major Prescott took it?"

"That's right, Russky. Pete is a nice fellow, but awfully security-conscious. He smelled something—not a harmless boy in need of help, but a dangerous foreigner being taken on a secret troop movement without proper clearance. And if he had gotten to you I'm not sure what would have happened. One wrong answer to any question, or even one bad reaction, and he might have decided to leave you in Colmar."

Pyotr shuddered. Those questions about Communism . . . But he had answered them honestly, and the questioner had not been tough Major Pete Prescott.

He said, "Sir, how did you learn of my case?"

"Oh, I just happened to be visiting a friend in G-3, and I heard Pete sputtering over in G-2. The thing that made him maddest was the fact that he's learned about you almost too late to pick you up." Captain Wilson laughed heartily. "I'd heard just enough about the boy called Russky to make me curious. So I volunteered to pick Russky up— and you know the rest."

Pyotr turned his head and studied Captain Wilson. That strange, glowing smile was back on his gaunt face. The captain was a wonderful man, but . . .

No, he thought, I *don't* know the rest!

"Sir," he said abruptly, "will you please tell me why you aren't wearing collar ornaments?"

Captain Wilson explored his collar.

"Well, well," he said. "That never happened before. Let's see, now. Oh, yes. My landlady washed one of my shirts yesterday, and I had to dress in a great rush this morning. So if she forgot to put the crosses back on—"

"*Crosses!*" Pyotr said.

"Yes, of course. I'm a chaplain."

"Oh."

"A Protestant chaplain, Russky."

"Oh."

"In fact, if you're Orthodox, as a proper Russian boy should be, I'm your chaplain."

"Oh."

"I was assigned to the 112th two weeks ago. I've held services at Horseshoe Green two Sundays in a row. Yet you've never seen me before. Now doesn't that seem a bit odd, Russky?"

"Odd, sir?"

Captain Wilson stopped Pyotr in the middle of the street. He fixed Pyotr with stern gray eyes.

"Young man," he said, "where were you last Sunday?"

Pyotr began to laugh. He laughed until his sides ached, and even the ache felt good.

"I've heard about your mess sergeant," Captain Wilson said. "He's a blasphemous old reprobate. He puts you on KP every Sunday, doesn't he?"

Pyotr nodded weakly.

"Then I'll tell him a thing or two!"

Pyotr shook his head.

"Please don't, sir. Cooking for the outfit is his form of godliness. Why, he's always singing hymns—" Pyotr gave one last glad laugh. "I'll come to chapel next Sunday, sir— and I'll bring Bellyrobber with me!"

Captain Wilson looked at the sky above, and sighed.

"Well, a mixed blessing is better than none," he said. "Now let's get rolling."

Chapter 13

ROUNDUP ON THE RHINE

Old Freihoffer stepped on the brake. His ancient charcoal-burning pickup truck groaned to a halt near the statue of Field Marshal Erich Friedrich Wilhelm von Ludendorff.

"Thank you very much for the ride, *mein herr*," Pyotr said, and jumped down to the curb.

"Have a pleasant day, Pyotr. Same time tomorrow?"

"Same time," Pyotr said. "*Auf wiedersehen.*"

He watched the smoke-belching truck rattle across Adolf Hitler Platz. Any day he wanted to come to town, all he had to do was wait on the road for Herr Freihoffer. The old man was a nice German. He hated to admit it, but he had met quite a few nice Germans lately. He sighed and began walking up tree-shaded Hermann Goering Strasse. It was a warm, sunny day in May, and by the time he reached Horst Wessel Strasse he felt hot and itchy under his winter-issue OD shirt. He rounded the corner, said "Hi" to the guard on the steps of the CP, and went inside. Down the hall, in the parlor, he found the Professor talking into a phone, and Nick Spiro sitting with his feet propped comfortably on the Charge of Quarters desk.

"Hi, Herr Censor," Nick said. "Seen any good Nazi movies lately?"

Pyotr nodded, smiling.

"I saw *The Baron Munchhausen* last night," he said. "It was in color—Technicolor, I believe you call it—and I must say it was amusing. For a German picture, that is."

Nick chuckled and picked up the CQ phone.

"I'll tell Green Three you're here," he said. "He should be free in a few minutes."

Pyotr settled down in a big leather lounge chair. He was nervous, as any boy would be who had an appointment with a colonel, but the cool dim parlor had a relaxing effect. He saw Nick close his eyes drowsily, so he watched the Professor. The staff sergeant's stripes on the Professor's sleeve looked new and a bit strange, but his telephone voice sounded smooth, confident. It was the voice of a key noncom, quietly, firmly in control of an important staff job.

Occupation duty, Pyotr thought. I just can't get used to it. Why, less than three months ago we were in Colmar. . . .

But Pyotr had left Colmar forever when he took that jeep ride with Captain Wilson. The division had assembled at Toul, then trucked to Boucq. After sleeping for three nights in the château of the Prince of Bourbon, Oboe Company piled into boxcars, and the long ride north began. Somewhere southeast of Aachen the freight trains halted and the journey continued in trucks to the end of a paved road. Then came a grim hike into the gloom of the Schleiden Forest. The terrain was dotted with concrete bunkers, crisscrossed with fire lanes, poisonous with saw-toothed tank barriers which the Germans called dragons' teeth. This was the second belt of the Siegfried Line.

Hellenthal, the strongpoint town, was ringed by enemy-held hills. It reminded the old-timers of Schmidt, the chief scene of grief during the terrible battle of the Hürtgen Forest, and the Germans' new rocket-launchers, the *Nebelwerfer*, filled the air with the howls of their "screaming meemies."

Later, Oboe made the "killer" march from Gemünd to Lommersdorf, sixteen hours of plodding through ankle-deep mud in pursuit of a German column that melted into nothingness before dawn. And still later Oboe reached the Rhine at Kärlich, a suburb of Koblenz.

There, miraculously, combat ended.

Machine gunners fished in the calm green waters. Captain Wilson baptized dozens of country-bred GIs in the Rhine, and earned the nickname "Holy Joe." Big, clumsy farm horses wandered into town. GIs of the neighboring Third Battalion rounded them up, saddled them, and staged a delightfully wacky "Rodeo on the Rhine" which received much publicity in *Stars and Stripes* as well as hundreds of newspapers in the States.

After bidding a fond farewell to Kärlich, Oboe rode across the Ernie Pyle Bridge, spent a week in reserve at Wirges, on the rim of the Ruhr pocket, and finally took a dead-of-night truck ride back across the Rhine and down to Rheinhessen Province. Once in its own occupation zone, the 28th Division spread out. The 112th Infantry occupied Worms, Alzey, Niederflörsheim-Dalsheim, and dozens of pretty villages which nestled in the rolling green countryside. For a while, jeep patrols roared up and down back roads, guarding great piles of abandoned German ammunition. For a while, officers fretted about "werewolves," the guerillas who, Hitler had promised, would harass the invaders to the bitter end. But the ammunition didn't need guarding, and there were no werewolves. The Rhineland Germans had had enough of war. While younger outfits drove to the Czech border to meet the Russians, the old Bloody Bucket basked in sunshine and peace.

Overcoats, field jackets and shoepacs belonged to the frostbitten past. The GIs had to turn in all ammunition, as well as the bolts of their rifles and carbines. Heavy "steels" gave way to light helmet liners. MAC Fritz's medics delivered German babies galore, and they proudly kept score like Air Corps aces, painting rows of tiny black swastikas on their helmets. A huge store of Wehrmacht liquor was "liberated," and on V-E night the celebrating antitank platoon happily swabbed down its guns with champagne. Greasegun Gannon became Captain Timothy X. Gannon. Nick Spiro moved over to S-3 as Operations Sergeant, the Professor took Nick's place as Intelligence Sergeant—and Pyotr was relieved of KP duty.

"The roads are crawling with DPs," Green Three said. "The labor camps are bulging with them. The first thing we've got to do is ship the French DPs across the border. We'll need a couple of interpreters in each truck convoy, and since you *parlez* French you're elected."

So Pyotr crossed the French border three times, fracturing the French language all the way. Between trips he censored German movies, making sure they did not contain Nazi propaganda. Since village theaters often were located above stables and barns, he could enjoy a variety of healthy farm odors along with the celluloid drama. But this morning a message had come from the battalion CP, saying that the colonel wanted to see him. So he had hitched a ride to Alzey, and here he was now, cooling his heels. . . .

The CQ phone rang. Nick Spiro answered it.

"Yes, sir," he said, nodding to Pyotr. "I'll send him in."

Pyotr marched across the parlor, opened the study door, advanced five paces, and snapped a formal "highball" salute at the officer behind the mahogany desk.

"Civilians don't salute," Green Three barked. "Sit down, Pribylov."

Douglas A. MacCampbell looked like a blond choirboy in an Ike jacket. He was a West Pointer, a light colonel at the age of twenty-eight. He ran his battalion with rare tactical skill, calculated ferocity, and occasional short rations of kindness. Today, rations were short indeed.

"Pribylov," he said, "we've run out of French DPs."

"Yes, sir," Pyotr said sadly.

"But Russian is your language, Pribylov. I am assigning you to the Russian DP team as of fourteen hundred this afternoon."

"You—you are, sir?"

"Do I detect a note of hesitancy in regard to this assignment, Pribylov?"

"Hesitancy, sir?"

"I've heard that you're afraid to go near fenced camps. Some nonsense about unfortunate experiences in the German labor force. Nothing to it, is there?"

Pyotr gulped.

"Well, Pribylov?"

"Nothing to it, sir. Nothing whatever."

"Good." Green Three leaned forward, crisply confidential. "As you know, most of the DPs in this area are bombed-out krauts. They're broke and hungry, but already halfway home. The others—the Poles, Balts, Russians, and so on—are our real problem. Most of them are housed in former farm labor camps. But hundreds more are still wandering around the countryside, raiding and stealing and generally making a nuisance of themselves." Green Three thumped the desk with his small hard fist. "I won't have it, Pribylov! I want those DPs rounded up and put in camps where they belong!"

"Yes, sir," Pyotr said.

"One stubborn group of Russians has forted up in an old factory near Worms. Camp Number Three is still half empty but for some reason they refuse to budge. We can't use force, or even threats. They're our allies. We've got to persuade them, Pribylov—actually *persuade* them to move to Camp Number Three!"

"Yes, sir," Pyotr said.

"I've got the best DP team in Occupied Germany," Green Three said, "but they have to work through an interpreter —or better still, Pribylov, a *diplomat*. Sergeant Rudenko was shipped home on rotation furlough last week. That leaves me with exactly one man in my command who can speak Russian that Russians can understand." Green Three jabbed his stiff index finger straight at Pyotr's startled eyes. "I mean *you*, Pribylov! Now, do you appreciate the importance of your mission?"

"Yes, sir!" Pyotr said.

"Then report to Captain Fritz at fourteen hundred sharp. That is all, Pribylov."

Pyotr stood up in good order, but tripped trying to step around his chair. He glanced over his shoulder and surprised Green Three in a mischievous choirboy grin. He slammed the door on his way out.

He told the Professor about it at noon chow, but indignation got him nowhere.

"So he gave you a GI sales pitch," the Professor said. "So what? Helping your own people, you'll soon get over being scared. And your mission *is* important. Why not take some pride in it?"

Pyotr reported to Captain Fritz at two o'clock sharp, but the MAC wasn't much help either.

"All I know," he said, "is that there are about a hundred of them, and they're all old folks. We'll have to find out the rest when we get there."

The short convoy of two jeeps and ten trucks cruised along the superhighway, or *Autobahn,* turned off on a side road, and parked in the main square of a little town. Pyotr's throat was sore. He had been trying, in his imagination, to imitate Bull Cotton's voice of command, and it still sounded like the shrill complaint of a sandpiper. He had composed and rehearsed a speech, and it had all the force of a nursery school toddler's plea for forbidden cookies. Now he wondered if he could speak at all.

The DP team consisted of Captain Fritz, medic; Captain Wilson, morale officer; Lieutenant Blodgett, operations and intelligence; Lieutenant Roget, supply; and one boy interpreter with paralyzed vocal cords. The team walked two blocks, and there was the factory—a big, grimy, bullet-

pocked brick building surrounded by a dirty girdle of cin-
ders.

The cinder wasteland was deserted. Obviously a lookout
had seen the Americans coming and given warning. MAC
Fritz led the way through a gutted machine shop into a
shipping room. Pyotr saw at a glance that the whole DP
colony had assembled. They stood in tight, defiant knots
among the hand trucks and stacks of cartons. For a moment
he thought they were all elderly, but then he spied young
faces and slim bodies here and there in the crowd. Boys
and girls his own age. Their parents were dead or missing
and grandparents were all they had left. But why had so
many old folk gathered in one place?

"Start talking," MAC Fritz whispered.

Pyotr stepped forward. His legs seemed to belong to
someone else. An old muzhik with a walrus mustache
moved forward also, as if to stop him. The head man, Pyotr
thought.

"Fellow Russians," he began, trying to sound like Bull.

The old muzhik smiled, lip curling. Pyotr heard sniggers.
He looked around desperately. A fat grandmother was sitting on the floor, nursing one knee. Then he noticed the
pattern of her peasant skirt, and realized his mistake.

"Fellow *Ukranians!*" he shouted in his normal boy's voice.
"My name is Pyotr, and I am from Kiev!"

A murmur swept through the crowd. The head man
stroked his mustache. Pyotr winked at him.

"How is your food supply?" he asked.

The head man did not answer.

"I'll tell you," Pyotr said. "You've been ransacking abandoned trains. You've been smashing shop windows and loot-
ing the shelves. You've survived, but just barely, day by
day. In another week you may be starving."

Still the old man did not answer. Pyotr nodded at the
fat woman on the floor.

"You have rheumatism, little mother. You are suffering."
He scanned the crowd coolly, deliberately, like Green
Three inspecting troops. "Many of you should be under a
doctor's care," he said. "Why do you refuse to enter a clean,
well-run American camp where you will receive such aid?"

He waited. The silence stretched painfully.

"Because the Americans are running dogs of the Soviets!"

Pyotr did not see the speaker. He heard the high, clear
young voice, and knew all he needed to know.

"The boy who spoke," he said, "learned that 'running dog'
insult in school. Such is the language of Communist propaganda. He uses their language even when he tries to fight
them. Yet he speaks for you, his elders. Before he went to
school he heard many times that once there was a better life
in a better Ukraine. Now he does not trust us because we
are wartime allies of the Soviets. He believes we are their
servants—'bootlicking lackeys' is the Party epithet. He
thinks we—"

"Why do you say 'we'?" the old muzhik asked suddenly.

For a moment Pyotr was confused. Then he laughed.

"I have been with the Americans so long," he said, "that
I think of myself as an American. In fact, I hope to become
an American citizen some day."

"Ah, so?" the head man said. "How did you happen to
meet the Long Legs in the first place, my fine young
boyar?"

"I was hoping you would ask that!" Pyotr said, and told
the story of his good fortune with the wonderful Long Legs
of Uncle Sam. He spoke as dramatically as he could, with
heroic flourishes, in the grand tradition of Russian storytell-
ers, and when he finished the old muzhik rocked his head
from side to side, rhythmically, in mock admiration.

"What do you think?" he asked the crowd.

There was much shaking of gray heads, and rubbing of

dry, wrinkled chins. Pyotr used the time to review what little he knew about Army DP operations.

"Will the Long Legs lock us in?" a rheumy voice inquired.

"The gate will be locked at night," Pyotr said, "to keep out thieves and men of violence. During the day it will be open."

"Will the Russians come and take us away?"

"No! The American Army will not allow it!"

"Are the Long Legs harsh with their prisoners?"

"I have already said that you will not be prisoners. The Army will provide food, clothing, shelter and medical aid, but each camp is run by the civilians who live in it, under the American system of democratic self-government. In a few months an international refugee organization called UNRRA will take over. And then there will be larger camps, more comforts, and the beginning of a better life for all of you."

The old muzhik stared steadily at Pyotr, hope battling with doubt in his faded blue eyes.

"The German SS decided we were too old to work," he said. "They gathered us together, crowded us into boxcars, and brought us here. They allowed us to keep our older grandchildren, but we were not fooled."

"You mean—"

"I think they planned to kill us and put the young ones to work. But the Americans were closing in, and there was a bombing raid, and the brave SS men ran away. Since then we've been free, but we can't go on like this." The old man shrugged wearily. "We have no reason to trust anyone, but if you will promise—"

"No, no, Grandfather!" that high, clear voice called from the crowd. "Make him prove he's from Kiev!"

"I'll prove it," Pyotr said. "Try me."

"What is the name of the biggest tiger in the zoo?"

Pyotr started to laugh, but sobered instantly.

"The Germans destroyed the animals in the zoo when they took Kiev," he said, "but in my day there were three tigers. I've forgotten the official name of the big one, but he was a magnificent animal from the jungles of Cooch Behar."

"He was not!" the boy shouted.

"Oh, yes he was," Pyotr said.

"Liar! He was from Bengal!"

Pyotr allowed the insult to linger in the air. Then he said, "The state of Cooch Behar is in Bengal. How do you suppose he got the nickname Coochy-Coochy?"

It took a while longer to persuade the DPs to leave behind their bedding and other useless baggage, but at last they were all in trucks, and Pyotr was in a jeep beside Captain Fritz, speeding toward Camp Number Three.

"Good work, Russky," the MAC said. "Judging from the sound and fury, you won a tough debate."

"It wasn't so tough," Pyotr said modestly.

"No? Not even when that girl started heckling you?"

"*Girl?*" Pyotr said.

"Sure, girl." MAC Fritz did a double-take. "Come to think of it, she was standing behind some people and she yelled like a boy. I guess you didn't spot her."

"What did she look like, sir?"

"Black eyes, black hair, sort of wild. Very un-Russian. In fact she looked like a Gypsy. A very cute, ornery little Gypsy."

Pyotr devoted several minutes to earnest meditation.

"You know," he said, "I think I'll stay in camp tonight and help those poor DPs get settled."

Chapter 14

Tanya didn't really look like a Gypsy. She was just a slim, saucy, fourteen-year-old Ukranian village girl who had inherited the dark prettiness of her Zaporozhe Cossack mother. Tanya wanted to be a woman before she got over being a tomboy. She was letting her lush black hair grow, but she hated the bother of combing it. The hair was wild, and so was Tanya.

"Hello, tiger," she said, bouncing into the chow line ahead of Pyotr. "Are we going berrypicking today, as you promised?"

"I promised no such thing, Tanya. I'm going to town."

She pouted. Pouting was a new tactic, and it worked better than temper tantrums.

"Always you go to town," she said.

"I have to keep up with the news," he said, and Tanya forgot all about tactics.

"You and your news!" she stormed. "It's making you sick —and it's making me sicker!"

Pyotr gritted his teeth. The chow line moved forward a few paces. He gave Tanya a push toward the mess hall door. Her eyes flashed a dark warning, and he knew that if he wanted a fight he could have one now.

Worse still, she was right. He had a small German radio in his Oboe Company billet near Worms, but for him the good jazz that came over the Armed Forces Network was just so much meaningless sound between news broadcasts. He spent most of his time here in Camp Number Three, because Green Three wanted him to and the DPs needed him, but each candlelit night without a radio was torture, and each morning he could not wait to get to Alzey to check on overnight developments. His whole future depended on the news, and the news was making him sick.

Once in the mess hall, he and Tanya carried their trays to a table near a window. Pyotr sat down and began to eat. Tanya sat down and began to cry.

"I'm s-s-sorry, Pyotr."

"I'm the one who should be sorry, Tanya. I pushed you."

"But I started it. I was jealous."

So that's it, Pyotr thought.

"I don't have a girl in town," he said gently.

"I know that, Pyotr. Girls always know such things."

"They do? How?"

She stomped her little boot under the table, then giggled because she had changed mood so quickly, then looked tragic to prove that she hadn't changed mood at all. Finally she gave up and just looked unhappy.

"You have a chance," she said. "I don't, and I'm jealous."

"But Tanya—"

"Some day the Russians will come with a train, and we'll all go back to the Ukraine."

"Tanya, I've told you a dozen times the Americans won't stand idly by and watch hundreds of people being forced into a train against their will."

"The Americans won't be there, Pyotr."

Pyotr stared at her. "What makes you say that?"

She smiled at him sadly, as if he were a small boy badly in need of guidance.

"The soldiers who bring our supplies talk freely among themselves. Drivers with time to kill read the *Stars and Stripes* and then throw their newspapers into trash cans. Some of our Czechs and Poles understand enough English to translate for the rest of us. So we know the Americans are leaving."

"Nonsense," Pyotr snapped. "Nobody knows what's going to happen. Not even the colonel."

"You see?" she said. "We know more than you do!"

Pyotr hung onto his temper. It wasn't easy, because he had been under a severe strain for weeks, and his nerves were raw.

The first anxiety had come when increasing numbers of old-timers began to go home for "rotation" furloughs. In theory, these battle-worn veterans would enjoy thirty days with their families, and then return to Germany. But the GIs said their return was unlikely. The old-timers had seen more than enough foreign service. After furlough, they would be held in the ZI, or Zone of the Interior, where they could teach combat lore to rookies in basic training.

Pyotr said good-by to Bellyrobber Bass, knowing he would never see the crusty old warrior again. And then the Army revealed its grand design for "redeployment"—the reshuffling of troops in the war against Japan.

Only four hundred thousand troops would be needed to occupy Germany, the *Stars and Stripes* reported. The rest of the three million men in the ETO, or European Theater of Operations, would either be shipped to the Pacific to fight the Japanese, or sent home for discharge from the service. Dischargees would be "phased out" according to a "point" system, and would make the trip home as soon as transports were available.

Pyotr said good-by to Stan Polski and Tubby Schmidt. And then he went to see the Professor.

"Will the point system break up the outfit?" The Professor repeated Pyotr's question and laughed. "Look, worrywart, to rate discharge, an *amerikaner Soldat* needs eighty-five points. He gets one point for each month of service in the States, and two points for each month of foreign service. He gets extra points for campaign stars, wounds and decorations. But in the Bloody Bucket that doesn't add up to much."

"It doesn't?" Pyotr said. "I should think a veteran unit would be full of high-point men."

The Professor shook his head somberly.

"The old 28th breathed its last in the Hürtgen Forest, Pete. We fellows who fought in the Bulge were replacements fresh out of basic training, led by a handful of Hürtgen survivors. We're combat veterans, but not the kind of old-timers who are eligible for discharge." The Professor allowed himself a wry grin. "I guess that makes us the *young* 28th. Anyway, most of us will be around to keep you company a year from now."

Pyotr prayed that it might be so, but a few days later he said good-by to Nick Spiro, and before the week ended the Armed Forces Network informed its GI listeners that the Army was about to name several divisions, now on occupation duty, which would see action in the Pacific.

"They won't be old divisions," the newscaster predicted, "but they won't be green either. They will be 'young-veteran' outfits, fresh yet combat-wise."

To Pyotr's sensitive ear, this had sounded like a shipping alert for the young 28th. He had pestered the Professor, but the Professor said, "No, Pete, the Army brass was born blind. They'll never look at the young personnel; they'll only look at the long combat record. And they'll keep our poor old Bloody Wheelchair in Germany 'til Kingdom Come."

Pyotr had believed it, or tried to, for a while. But this morning, as he toyed with his breakfast in the mess hall of Camp Number Three, he couldn't pretend any longer. He peeked at Tanya. She was just sitting there, smiling.

"All right," he said, "I'll admit there's a slim chance that the 28th will be leaving."

"I didn't say anything about your precious 28th, Pyotr. I said the Americans will be leaving."

Pyotr choked over his cocoa.

"You mean leaving Germany? All of them?"

"Of course not, silly. I mean leaving this province. Two weeks from now it will be part of the French Occupation Zone."

Pyotr tried to appear unruffled, but that maddening smile of Tanya's made it impossible.

"Rumors," he growled. "New DPs come into camp and spread the latest gossip. That's all you've got to go on, Tanya. You pulled that French Zone rabbit out of the same hat that produced the terrible Russian kidnap train—"

"It's not a thing to sneer about, Pyotr. Already they're forcing people to go back home."

She was completely sincere now, and afraid. Pyotr could see it. But what about the Russian trains that rumbled through Alzey every day, gaily decorated with leafy boughs and green foliage? Surely the DPs going home in those long freight trains were happy.

And yet, sometimes the DP grapevine was magically accurate. Tanya just might be right—again.

"Pyotr."

He sighed. "Yes, Tanya."

"Are you angry?"

He eyed her closely. She was a little girl again, about to begin wheedling. He swallowed a last mouthful of dehydrated eggs and stood up.

"I'm not angry," he said, "and when I come back from town we'll go berrypicking."

She followed him to the gate, chattering, but he managed to reach the autobahn in time to hitch a ride with Herr Freihoffer. He dropped off at Adolf Hitler Platz, murmured *"Guten tag"* to the saucy robin which was perched on Field Marshal von Ludendorff's *Pickelhaube*—a funny-sounding word for spiked helmet—and walked toward Hermann Goering Strasse. Halfway up the street he heard motors behind him. He turned his head and saw a column of trucks coming on fast with canvas tops down. Two men shouted greetings. He waved, and then he recognized faces. These men were from the 112th Infantry, and they were coming back from Bains-les-Bains.

Bains-les-Bains was a little resort town across the French border. Before the war it had been a spa, a popular "watering place" where vacationing French businessmen had eased their tired bones in the hot baths. A month ago, General Cota had established a 28th Division rest center in Bains-les-Bains, and since then hundreds of Keystone GIs had enjoyed five-day passes there. But the men in this convoy had left Alzey only two days ago. Now they were returning three days ahead of time, arriving in the morning. The trip from Bains-les-Bains took thirteen hours, so that meant they had traveled all night.

Pyotr broke into a run.

The convoy had parked on Horst Wessel Strasse, and the Green Battalion men were leaping out of the trucks, mingling with GIs who had come pouring out of the billets. The street pulsed with noise, with animal vigor and excitement. Pyotr ran on, toward the CP, sweating, gasping, because this was a hot day in June and his own excitement was almost choking him. Jeeps lined the curb in front of the comfortable old brick house. Several officers came rushing out of the front door. They piled into jeeps and roared away, but not before Pyotr had glimpsed the tough, wiry figure of Gustin M. Nelson, the fiery little chicken colonel who had led the 112th from Schmidt to the Rhine.

The Old Man, he thought. He came all the way from Regiment. This is it! Now we'll roll on!

He paused on the stone steps.

I won't be with them, he thought, and a dull sickness took his excitement from him.

He opened the heavy oaken door and stepped into the

cool hall. A few more steps, and he stood in the parlor. There was the Professor, sitting at the CQ desk, talking quietly into a telephone as always. He scarcely knew Pat Dunphy, the new Operations Sergeant, but the burly non-com had a voice like a train announcer.

"Yes, sir," Pat said, "it's official. No, I don't know when, but it'll be this week."

This was no time to bother the Professor. Pyotr backed into the hallway. He left the house.

Outside, the sun seemed to singe him. He walked down the garden path, pushed open the iron gate, and entered the courtyard. Penned geese honked at him. Fat rabbits stirred lazily in their hutches, then fell asleep again. He passed the stable and stepped into the coach house.

The coach house kitchen served three companies, sending chow out to the various occupied villages by truck. But only one cook was on duty now, a fellow from Nan Company. One cook, and a boy whom everyone called Little Polski. Little Polski was holding a potato in one hand and a paring knife in the other. Not paring, not moving, just staring into space.

"Where is everybody?" Pyotr asked.

"They goofed off," the cook said. "The news come in and they quit work, that's all."

"Where did they go, please?"

"Oh, the new clubhouse, I guess." The Nan cook grunted. "Come to think of it, why am I here?"

He hung his apron on a peg and walked out. Pyotr turned to Little Polski. "Where is the 28th going?" he asked loudly.

Little Polski blinked.

"They kept saying 'CBI,'" he said, "but I don't know what 'CBI' means."

Pyotr frowned. "CBI" stood for China-Burma-India The-

ater of Operations, but soldiers in Europe used it casually
to indicate any area in the Pacific.

"Take a walk, Little Polski," he said. "It will relieve your
feelings."

Little Polski began to cry.

"Your fate is no worse than mine," Pyotr said, but Little
Polski did not hear him. Stan had taken this pale, stunted
boy into the kitchen because he was a Polish war orphan.
Bellyrobber had tried to fatten him up. Now Stan and
Bellyrobber were gone. Soon Chuck and Mario would go,
and Little Polski would be alone.

"Come with me," Pyotr said.

Little Polski started to stand up. The slick, half-peeled
potato slipped from his fingers. He sat watching it roll
away, and then he threw the paring knife to the floor and
covered his face with his hands. His broken sobs followed
Pyotr to the door.

"When you are finally alone," he said, "come to the
camp. I'll take care of you, Little Polski."

The "new" clubhouse was a huge, hideous, castle-like
pile that had been built by a newly rich merchant baron
in the 1920s. The GIs had cleaned and decorated its cav-
ernous rooms with loving care, and today, as Pyotr dragged
his feet up Bismarck Strasse, he could hear them singing.
They were singing "Old Soldiers Never Die," the sweet, sad
regimental song of the 112th Infantry. He stood under a
shade tree and listened for a while, but he did not go into
the clubhouse. It would be too crowded, too noisy, too full
of vigorous young men who imagined they wanted nothing
more than to go home to a life of peaceful civilian routine,
but actually were thrilled by the prospect of more excitement, more movement, more danger in distant, unknown
lands.

I would be a ghost at the feast, he thought. We have
come at last to a parting of the ways.

He walked slowly to Adolf Hitler Platz and sat down on a bench. When we came here three months ago, he thought, Green Three wanted to tear down the street signs, but Division wouldn't let him. Wait for Military Government, they said; it's MG's job to change street names. But MG still hasn't taken over, and this is still Adolf Hitler Platz. Next week the French will march in and wonder what we've been doing with our time.

A supply truck coasted out of Goebbels Strasse. Pyotr waved and the driver picked him up. Once inside Camp Number Three he headed straight for his barracks, but he saw a slim, nimble figure detach itself from the crowd of women around the washtubs. Tanya had spied him. Now she was running toward him. He hurried into the barracks, climbed the stairs, and entered his cadre room. He threw himself down on his bunk and closed his eyes.

"Pyotr!" Tanya's high, clear tomboy voice called. "Pyotr, you promised to take me berrypicking!"

If I just lie here with my eyes closed, he thought, I can pretend it is night. If I pretend long enough it really will be night, and then perhaps I can sleep.

"Pyotr!" Tanya called, louder now. "Pyotr, I know you're up there hiding!"

If I could only sleep now, he thought. Sleep is like a little death, and I would welcome it.

"Pyotr! You *promised!*"

A snort of laughter burst from Pyotr's lips. He sat up, astonished that he could laugh. He swung his legs off the bunk, got up, and went to the window. Tanya glared up at him, wild-haired, furiously angry, and totally alive.

"What's all the fuss about?" he growled. "Just hold your horses and I'll be down in a minute."

Chapter 15

OLD SOLDIERS NEVER DIE

The slanting rays of the setting sun spotlighted the jeep at the camp gate. Pyotr recognized the Professor at the wheel, but who was that big officer sitting beside him?

He lengthened his stride, then slowed down again.

"Oh, for heaven's sake!" Tanya said. "Give me the berry basket and run on ahead!"

He did just that. Fifty yards from the jeep he began to whoop like a Red Indian. He was still whooping when Bull Cotton enveloped him in a bear hug.

"A second lieutenant," he said when he regained his breath. "I can't believe it, Bull."

"Neither can I," Bull said. "But Greasegun says I'll get over it, like a case of measles."

"I thought you were still recuperating at the 95th General Hospital in Bar-le-Duc," Pyotr said. "What happened?"

"Oh, I got tired of being penned up in a ward, so they let me go legally before I went AWOL. They even gave me a week to kick around in before I reported for duty, so I headed for Bains-les-Bains. That's where I was when the news came through that the 28th was going to roll." Bull grinned reflectively. "I saw the boys boarding trucks for the ride back to Germany, so I knew what I had to do. When I checked in at the CP Green Three said, 'Give me your overseas cap,' and I did. He pulled a gold bar out of his desk and pinned it on the cap. So now I'm an officer and a gentleman by Act of Congress."

"It's odd that I missed you this morning," Pyotr said. "I saw the Bains-les-Bains convoy twice on my way to the CP."

"I yelled at you twice," Bull said, "but you just kept on going like a big-bottomed bird." He whacked Pyotr on the shoulder and almost knocked him down. "But we're squared away now, kiddo—and you're going to have dinner with us tonight."

"Us?" Pyotr said, and looked at the Professor.

"Us," the Professor said, with a wink. "In the officers' quarters yet!"

The door opened. Bull Cotton barked "tensh-hut!" as the colonel stepped into the room.

"At ease," Green Three said. "Remain seated, gentlemen."

He strode briskly toward the littered dining table. He handed a brown envelope to Pyotr.

"Here," he said, "is the record of your service with my battalion. I am told that you plan to seek employment with the U. S. Army in Europe. If you do, be sure to present these papers. They recommend you without reservation. They also mention the fact that I shall consider myself honored if you choose me to serve as one of your sponsors for citizenship."

Pyotr fumbled with the envelope. He didn't know how to respond fully, so he said:

"Thank you, sir—and best of luck in the CBI."

The colonel smiled a small secret smile.

"I have the feeling," he said, "that we'll be closer to the home islands of Japan. But one more thing, Russky. I talked to Major Deschamps, the French liaison officer, a while ago. He has guaranteed that no DP trains will leave this area without a thorough check. Only DPs who want to go home will go home." He clucked thoughtfully. "I believe that covers everything. Good-by, Russky, and good luck."

He shook Pyotr's hand and walked out.

"Whew!" Bull said. "He really lays it on the line, don't he? I mean, doesn't he?"

Everybody laughed.

"I think we'd better do likewise," MAC Fritz said. "Shall I proceed, gentlemen?"

Everybody nodded.

"All right," the MAC said. "It's like this, Russky. We don't know the exact day we'll roll, but it'll be very soon. We'll be processed at Camp Pittsburgh, near Reims, France, and then wait for a ship in the hedgerow country near Le Havre. We'll land in the States in late July or early August, take a month's rest and recuperation leave, and then report for about two months of training with new tactics and weapons. Finally we ship out to the Pacific. There's no real secret involved in any of this, so you may as well know the score."

MAC Fritz sipped coffee from his elegant Dresden china cup and set the cup down on the snowy white linen table-cloth.

"Only God knows what it's going to be like in the Pacific, Russky—but each of us has resolved that if he comes through alive he'll do everything in his power to bring you over to the United States."

Pyotr looked at their faces—the faces of MAC Fritz, Bull Cotton, Greasegun Gannon, Holy Joe Wilson, and the Professor—and he sat very still, feeling his throat tighten.

"We'll keep in touch by letter," MAC Fritz said. "We'll be off in some isolated combat area, but we do have families and friends in the States. I have two uncles who practice law. Tim has political connections that reach from Boston to Washington. Joe knows bishops. The Professor has an in with do-gooder organizations in New York. Bull is up for the Distinguished Service Cross, and some Kentucky congressman is going to have his arm twisted. In other words, Russky, we're going to put our civilian auxiliaries to work, and if you can keep your head above water in Germany, we'll bring you home."

He drummed his plump fingers on the tablecloth.

"Anybody got anything to add?"

"Yeah," Bull said. "Before we leave we ought to set him up in a camp in the American Zone."

"I disagree," Captain Wilson said. "He'll be all right here for a while, with Major Deschamps to look in on him from time to time, and we know how to get in touch with him here. If he moved we might lose contact."

"That makes sense," Greasegun Gannon said. "Once things are more settled and the occupation outfits are stationed in permanent sectors, he can apply for work in the U. S. Zone. But until then I think he should stand pat."

Pyotr nodded gratefully in all directions. He cleared his throat and managed one husky word:

"Why . . . ?"

"We got together this afternoon," MAC Fritz said. "We decided that we couldn't live with ourselves if we let you down. You're one of us, boy. That's why."

Pyotr looked away from the kind blue eyes. Then he noticed that Captain Wilson's head was bowed, as if in prayer. He stared fixedly at a crack in the floor.

"Well, dinner's done," Bull said loudly. "Want to go visit the boys at the clubhouse, Russky?"

Pyotr shook his head, still trying not to break down.

"The officers are throwing a party an hour from now," Bull said. "You're too young for a shindig like that, and I'm way too clumsy. So why don't we take a run over to Oboe Company—"

"Hold it!" Greasegun said. "You can't back out of the party, Bull. You're an *officer*. And besides, there's a little nurse from the Evac Hospital I want you to meet. She . . ."

His voice trailed off, perhaps because the Professor had stood up suddenly.

"It's been a delightful evening, gentlemen," the Professor said very formally, "but since you must prepare for your party I think it is time for the enlisted men to withdraw." He bowed from the hips. "Coming, Pete?"

Without waiting for an answer, he took Pyotr by the arm. Pyotr stood up feeling oddly shaky. Captain Wilson's bony hand closed around his own, then MAC Fritz's, then Greasegun's, then Bull's. The Professor led him through the doorway and down the hall. He tripped over something but the Professor held him up. And then they were out under the stars, and the night air felt cool against his hot, wet face.

The ride to Camp Number Three was wordless, strained. The Professor parked ten yards from the gate. He opened the breast pocket of his Ike jacket.

"Here," he said, "are our home addresses and the names and addresses of our closest relatives."

Pyotr took the slip of paper. The Professor reached under the waistband of his jacket. When his hand reappeared, it held something that gleamed dully in the lantern light from the gate.

"We were supposed to turn in all weapons," the Professor said, "but I kept one souvenir. Take it."

Pyotr's fingers closed on the grip of a pistol. This was no cheap wartime P-38. This was a prewar Reichswehr Lüger, an aristocrat among officers' pistols. He felt a guilty thrill as he slipped it under his belt.

"I told you we were sure to stay on occupation duty," the Professor said, "because I didn't want to worry you. Now the time for games is past. This camp may be safe, and Greasegun's advice about not moving until things settle down may be good. But if trouble starts, Pete, don't hesi-

tate. Take off fast and head for the nearest American outfit."

"And the Lüger, Professor?"

"It's oiled and loaded and you know how to fire it. But
there's an old Army rule about sidearms I want you to remember. Never pull a gun just to bluff. When you pull a
gun—"

"I'll remember," Pyotr said.

"One more thing, then. My mother is a widow. My sisters got married and left home. So when you come to the
States, why don't you move in with Mother and me?"

Surprise smashed into Pyotr's middle like an invisible
fist. He almost stopped breathing.

"It'll be a favor to me, Pete. I need a master's degree,
so I'll be in class or the library most of the time. Mother
will be lonesome and you can keep her company. And don't
worry about dietary laws. We haven't kept a kosher table
since Dad died."

Pyotr filled his chest with air. He said, "Professor, if you
only knew what a home means to me—"

"Cut the mush," the Professor said. "Your girl is standing
in the shadows beyond the gate."

Tanya was a slim dark blur against the peeling white
paint of the old barracks. She had heard him out in silence,
and still she did not move or speak.

"So I seem to have a chance after all," he said uncom-
fortably. "What do you think, Tanya?"

She stirred slightly.

"You will always have a chance, Pyotr."

Pyotr frowned into the darkness. He often had the feeling that she was older than he, that she knew things he
would never know, that in any argument she was bound to
be right. This morning she had said that he had a chance,
and she didn't. Now she was saying that he would always

have a chance. He supposed he ought to accept it as a fine tribute to his male superiority, but somehow he couldn't.

"What do you mean by that?" he asked.

"You make your own chances, Pyotr. You think, you feel, and then you act."

"But so do you, Tanya. You're as active as a filly."

"Ah, yes. A filly in a fence field. I frisk about, but I never quite jump the fence." She gave a small feminine sniff of laughter. "But you! No matter where you are, no matter how bad things seem, you keep trying. No fence can hold you— even if you are as witless as a colt."

Pyotr nodded, unseen. Jealousy still lurked beneath her wisdom, and it showed. But he must be gentle tonight.

"You'll have your chance too," he said. "The French will protect you from the Russians."

"It isn't just a matter of force, Pyotr. Persuasion will be enough for most of our people. They're tired of struggling, tired of waiting. The future has no shape at all, but they remember the black earth. Even under the Soviets the Ukraine is their home. So in the end they will go home."

"That doesn't mean you have to go."

"If Grandfather goes, I must go," Tanya said. "I am all he has left, Pyotr."

Pyotr wondered what he could do or say to help her. Maybe if he just changed the subject. Anything that would interest a girl . . .

"Did I mention," he said, "that the officers are giving a party tonight?"

"No, you didn't."

"Their guests will be nurses," he said.

"Oh! Are they pretty?"

"Very pretty. American girls are all tall and blond and long-legged," he added teasingly.

The small blur of Tanya straightened against the wall.

"What will they wear, Pyotr?"

"Evening gowns, of course."

"And will there be dancing?"

"Certainly. The colonel engaged an orchestra from Mann-heim, so it will be quite a *soigné* affair."

Tanya sighed, and Pyotr had a sudden vision of Bull Cotton towering over a short, squat, homely brunette in an Army nurse's blouse. He heard the Victrola needle bump over a groove in the ancient fox-trot record. He heard the rubber soles of Bull's Size 14 combat boots squeal on the floor as the dancing couple turned. He saw the homely nurse make a face—and then, mercifully, the vision vanished.

"I wish we could be there watching," he said.

"I wish we could be there dancing," Tanya replied softly.

Now, Pyotr thought. *Now!*

He took a step forward. He felt a small hand press against his chest, and he stopped.

"Good night, tiger," Tanya purred, and her little feet pattered away toward the women's barracks.

Pyotr grinned ruefully. It took so much planning, so much courage to kiss a girl. Still, he had made her happy for a moment, and he would kiss her yet.

I ought to hit the sack now, he thought. But I won't.

He walked aimlessly, and he came to the barbed-wire fence, and he stood looking up into the starry sky. In a few days, a week at the most, the 28th would roll on, leaving him behind. There would be trips to town, and formal fare-wells, but he felt that the real good-bys already had been said. He looked toward the west, toward Alzey, and in his mind's eye he saw the doughboys gathered at the oaken tables of the clubhouse. They were singing "Old Soldiers Never Die."

It was a sad, sentimental, romantic song, and if the wrong ears heard it, the words might sound false. But the lyrics had been written by the bandmaster of the 112th Infantry many years ago, in honor of the aging veterans of the Civil War, and they truly saluted all old soldiers whose wars were done. The Keystone GIs of World War II had taken the song to their hearts.

The strong young voices came to Pyotr faintly, as if from far, far beyond the clubhouse, and then they faded away. He listened, straining, but all he heard was the squeal of hinges as the camp gate closed for the night. There was a thump of wood, a rattling of chains, a click as the key turned in the lock. For a moment the old smothering sensation came back. He straightened his shoulders and cast it off. He walked back toward the barracks, and already he seemed to be living in memory.

Defiantly, under his breath, he sang, "Old soldiers never die, they just fade away. . . ."

Chapter 16

A BAND OF BROTHERS

The sound came in the heart of night, in the deep darkness before dawn. Pyotr opened his eyes. He listened to the huff-puff of the locomotive, the hiss of steam. Couplings crashed hollowly as the long line of freight cars came to a halt on the siding. He rolled out of his bunk.

Leon Anatote, who shared the cadre room with him, awoke and said shakily, "Is it the Russian train?"

"It is," Pyotr said. He finished dressing. He shrugged into his field jacket, put on his overseas cap, reached under the bunk and pulled out his old-fashioned roll-pack, which wise GIs preferred to the newer, heavier "cargo" pack. He did not say good-by to Leon. He found a group of men gathered around the stairwell, but when they spoke to him he did not answer. He ran downstairs and headed for the women's barracks. People were pouring into the street now, talking wildly. He plowed through them, knocking larger bodies aside with ruthless speed and drive.

"Pyotr!"

The call came from an upstairs window. He waited, holding his pack by one strap. Tanya popped through the door, a quick little shadow in some kind of billowing garment. She rushed toward him, then stopped uncertainly.

"Well, they timed it right," he said. "After the Americans left, and before the French arrived."

"Yes," Tanya said, and nothing more.

"You can still go with me," he said. "There is time to

dress. I have everything we need, and I won't make any mistakes."

"No, Pyotr."

"All right, then. Please take care of Little Polski."

"I will, Pyotr."

He gathered himself together.

"Good-by, Tanya," he said. "I'll never forget—"

Suddenly she was in his arms, a tiny girl in a flannel bathrobe that had been made for a large woman. She was so soft, so pliant, yet so strangely full of life and strength. He felt her lips against his, and then she whispered fiercely, "Beat them, tiger, beat them!" and raced back into the barracks.

Pyotr stared blindly after her, realizing with dumb amazement that she had won again. Now, truly, he would never forget her.

He shook himself like a dog emerging from water. He sped toward the stretch of fence that was farthest from the railroad siding. He threw his pack over the top, scrambled up the mesh. His trousers caught on the topmost strand. He cleared the snag and dropped to the ground.

For two hundred yards he ran full tilt through smooth meadowland. He cut to the left, then, and came out on the side road. The road guaranteed safe running for another ten minutes, and he did not slow down until he saw the dim bulk of the trees which screened the autobahn. The trees loomed up directly ahead, so he stopped. He listened, and heard voices.

The voices must belong to guards who had been posted to keep fugitives from reaching the autobahn. They were talking freely because they did not expect any fleeing DPs to arrive so soon. All he had to do now was work his way around them. He turned, meaning to cross the ditch and steal into the field, and then a voice said, "You, there—stay right where you are."

Pyotr reached under his belt but made no other movement. The man was coming from the direction of the camp, which meant that he had made a short patrol down the road and was returning to the guard post among the trees. Pyotr waited patiently, and at last the short, square body took shape before him.

"What are you doing here?" the man said.

Pyotr swung his arm up, over, and down. The barrel of the Lüger landed with a soft thud. Too soft. The man screamed and sank to his knees.

Pyotr reached out, groping, and touched cloth. He brushed the cap off the man's head and swung hard at the spot where the cap had been. This time the pistol barrel bit in, hard and true.

I hope I haven't killed him, Pyotr thought, and straightened up, again waiting patiently. He had to wait, for if he hid they would search until they found him, and if he ran they would pursue until they ran him to earth.

Feet pelted in the dry dust of the road. Pyotr could not see the men, but his ears gave him all the range-sensing he needed. He leveled the Lüger, fired, let the beautiful balance bring the piece back into the target area, and blasted off four nicely spaced shots.

A shriek of pain mingled with the last sharp crack of the pistol. There was a deep-voiced oath, then silence. The unwounded guard had stopped to aid his comrade.

Pyotr tucked the Lüger in his belt, calculated the number of shots he had left, and dogtrotted across the fields. After covering about two miles he decided to try the autobahn again. He sat down and rested. Dawn came. A wide ribbon of concrete stretched toward the horizon, gray and empty in this land of no gasoline and no civilian cars.

He put on his pack and began walking.

An Army truck sped by, but he didn't respond to the yell from the cab. He had a map, blankets, and strong legs, and he didn't want a ride. In a day or so he would reach the nearest American outfit. There were lots of American outfits, and somewhere along the line he would find what he sought —useful work, freedom, and a sense of belonging.

I'm walking too fast, he thought.

He hooked his thumbs under his pack straps and settled down to what the Army called a route step. When he had first seen it, the route step had looked more like a shuffling slouch than a proper military pace, but it ate up the miles and the GIs swore by it. If you had guts and endurance besides, they said, the old slop-step would sure as hell get you there.

The sun rose, red and hot. He began to sweat. He wiped the sweat from his eyes and began to sing "Old Soldiers." He was all alone on a deserted highway, and there was no one to see that he marched with a band of brothers.

S/Sgt Irving P. Lindner
ASN 32528601
Hq Co 4th Bn 112th Inf
28th Inf Div
Camp Shelby, Miss.

September 30, 1945

Dear Pete:

Thanks for the wonderful letter.

Mother forwarded it to me from New York, and I am delighted to learn that you've secured a good job with the 1st Division. Reading between the lines, I suspect that you had a wee bit of trouble ducking out of Camp Number Three, but we can take that up when we meet again.

And we will meet again, Pete. Considering the miracles that have happened already, I don't doubt it for a minute. Just look:

On August 3 we landed in Boston. On August 6 they dropped the A-Bomb. And on August 14 I was in Times Square, celebrating V-J Day. After that chain-reaction, I'll believe anything!

Here at Camp Shelby, the old 28th is breaking up at last. The point system means nothing; there's no more war for us to fight, and they're discharging us in droves. Two months from now we'll all be back in civilian clothes. It's a little sad, seeing a great outfit melt away, but after all most of us are civilians at heart and I don't plan to cry much when they hand me my discharge papers.

As you probably know, Bull is staying in as a Regular, but MAC Fritz and Holy Joe and Greasegun are already out there in mufti, pitching for you, and when I get home I'll be working right along with them. . . .

Pyotr D. Pribylov
c/o Special Troops
APO 1, US Zone
Germany

December 22, 1945

Dear Professor:

My hand is shaking like a leaf, but I've *got* to write to you. President Harry Truman's Christmas Proclamation just came over the radio. We were decorating the tree when we heard it. A Latvian DP woman who was helping us fainted dead away. I can just imagine what it's like in the DP camps. They must be wild with excitement.

Actually, of course, 40,000 DPs aren't very many for a great nation like the United States to absorb, but it's a beginning, and I'm told that the Government may admit a larger number next year. Not that I want to wait until next year—I'm keeping my fingers crossed, hoping I'll be one of the lucky ones in the first 40,000. I understand that the CIC will screen all applicants for citizenship, but considering the wonderful sponsors I can count on, it seems to me that I really do have a better chance than most.

They say shipments will begin in March. . . .

MARCH 15, 1946

PYOTR D. PRIBYLOV
C/O SPECIAL TROOPS
APO 1, US ZONE
GERMANY

EVERYTHING SET WELCOMING COMMITTEE WILL
MEET SHIP AT DOCK

THE PROFESSOR

ABOUT THE AUTHOR . . .

George Armor Sentman was born and raised in Maryland, and educated at the University of Missouri. During World War II he served more than three years in the Army, earning his Combat Infantry Badge with the 28th Division, around which this story is built. Since the war, Mr. Sentman has been a writer and editor in New York City. Before *Russky*, he wrote many short stories and the very successful book *Drummer of Vincennes.*